Hope sat up in her bed with a gasp.

She bent her knees, hugging them to her in the loneliness of her room.

In her dreams, Eric had been kissing her again. And she'd been kissing him back. The way it had always been with them. Mutual love. Equal longing.

She'd had this dream too many times to count, reliving the time when she and her husband were still together.

She'd loved Eric Granston nearly all her life. The boy he'd been. The man he'd become.

And she loved him still.

There was a place in her heart only Eric could fill.

Hope sighed, recalling her feelings from the night they'd parted. Her sense of being right.

She hadn't realized that being "right" could feel so wrong....

Books by Kathryn Alexander

Love Inspired

The Reluctant Bride #18
A Wedding in the Family #42
The Forever Husband #78

KATHRYN ALEXANDER

writes inspirational romance because, having been a Christian for many years, she felt that incorporating the element of faith in the Lord into a romantic story line was a lovely and appropriate idea. After all, in a society where love for a lifetime is difficult to find, imagine discovering it, unexpectedly, as a gift sent from God.

Married to Kelly, her own personal love of a lifetime, Kathryn and her husband have one son, John, who is the proud owner of the family's two house *pests,* Herbie the cat and Copper the dog.

Kathryn and her family have been members of their church for nearly five years, where she co-teaches a Sunday school class of active two-year-olds. She is now a stay-at-home mom who writes between car pooling, baby-sitting and applying bandages, when necessary.

The Forever Husband
Kathryn Alexander

Love Inspired®

Published by Steeple Hill Books™

STEEPLE HILL BOOKS

Steeple
Hill™

ISBN 0-373-87078-7

THE FOREVER HUSBAND

Visit us at www.steeplehill.com

Printed in U.S.A.

For if our heart condemn us, God is greater than
our heart, and knoweth all things.
—*I John* 3:20

To Anne Canadeo,
editor extraordinaire.
Thank you for three beautiful books!

Prologue

Eric smiled at his wife and extended an arm to take her hand in his protective grasp, then pulled her gently into the boat with him. Hope had been watching from the sidelines, uncertain about joining her husband in the anchored, but unsteady vessel. But as he urged her into testing their new purchase, she came haphazardly into his arms with nervous laughter and, finally, a shriek sounding of certain catastrophe when the boat rocked sharply.

"Eric! Do something! We're tipping over!"

His grip on her arms was as firm as it could be without hurting, and he steadied her before she slid her own desperate arms around his waist.

His smile was wide. "Don't be afraid, Hope. You know how to swim if you need to."

"But we'll probably both drown because I'll be

too scared to let go of you! If this thing tips, we're going down *together*," she warned.

Eric laughed out loud, the sound of his voice mingling with the slap of water against the boat's hull. On a sudden gust of October wind a swirl of autumn leaves blew from the lakeshore into the boat and around their feet.

"We're going down together, huh?" Eric repeated in a solemn tone.

Hope loosened her clinging hold on him slightly, and tilted her head back in time to see the laughter fade from her husband's eyes. Just then, the boat steadied some, although that did little to ease the rapid pace of Hope's heart as she stared into the depths of Eric's darkening gaze.

"Yes, you're going with me," she responded with a teasing smile. Then, lifting her hand to his chest, she touched the soft fabric of his shirt and watched Eric's gaze lower to her mouth. He would kiss her; he always did when he had that look. But the waiting wasn't easy, even after all the years.

"That's where I want to be, Hope. With you...always." His hands moved upward into her windblown hair, and he leaned toward her, as Hope raised herself up to meet his kiss. Eric's warm mouth moved firmly against hers, taking and giving—both of them wanting more of the love they'd found in each other's arms....

Hope woke up instantly, sitting up in her bed

with a gasp. She pulled her knees up, hugging them to her in the loneliness of her room.

Eric had been kissing her again, and she'd been kissing him back—as it had always been with them. Mutual love; equal longing. She gave a soft sigh. She'd had this dream too many times to count. And it wasn't a dream in the true sense of the word. Not fantasy or a capricious imagination at work in a sleep-filled mind. It was real. A clearly remembered incident replayed in her sleep. Over and over. A relived moment in time from when she and her husband had lived together. She'd loved Eric Granston nearly all her life—the boy he had been, the man he'd become. And she loved him still. There was a place in her heart only Eric could fill.

Chapter One

"Eric? What are you doing here?" Hope had walked around the corner of a French-fry stand, surprised to find her dark-haired husband. She hadn't expected him at this annual hospital fund-raiser.

"I came to see my girl." With a smile, he reached down to pick up their six-year-old daughter, Beth, who had grinned broadly as she rushed into her father's arms.

"Hi, Daddy. I'm glad you're here. Maybe you could win me a goldfish."

"No goldfish, sweetheart. They never live long, and it breaks your heart when they die," Eric replied before returning his attention to Hope. "I was upstairs visiting Cassie, and she told me that you were down here at this carnival, so I thought I'd stop by to see Beth." He paused. "You don't mind, do you? I mean, I realize it's not my regularly scheduled day to see her."

"No," Hope said with a shake of her head. The wind caught her blond hair, blowing it around her face; she pushed it back. "I don't mind. I'm just surprised to see you."

She was *very* surprised, in fact, considering she and Eric had barely spoken since their separation six months ago. Exchanging children for visitation had been the extent of their involvement with each other until recently, when their older daughter, Cassie, had been hospitalized with pneumonia. Since then they'd seen each other more often, but their encounters remained brief, consisting mostly of passing each other coming and going from the hospital room, and discussing Cassie's improving condition when necessary. Basically, they avoided each other as much as possible. Actually, Hope had to admit, Eric was the one doing most of the avoiding, which was probably for the best if she was to have any chance of getting him out of her heart.

"What are you doing here, anyway? Trying to keep this daughter of ours entertained?" he asked with a teasing pull on Beth's blond ponytail.

"Something like that," Hope replied. "I thought this little carnival would be fun for her."

Eric nodded. "And are you having fun yet?" he asked the little girl wearing a yellow blouse and matching jumper with decorative sunflowers on the front pockets. Beth was a beautiful child, Eric thought for the millionth time. She looked just like her mother.

"Yeah! Look at those stuffed animals over there, Dad." Beth pointed to a row of booths offering various games and prizes. "The one where you throw darts at the balloons can win a fat green frog."

"Living or stuffed?" Hope asked immediately. She didn't like the idea of a backyard funeral for a deceased frog later in the week. Or worse yet, the thing might actually live.

"Stuffed, Mom. Why would I want a real frog? They're too yucky to have for a pet."

"Good. I've trained you well," Hope remarked, and saw the flash of amusement in her husband's dark gaze.

"Let's go see if we can win one, Beth," Eric suggested. Then he looked directly into his wife's blue eyes, something he had resisted doing whenever possible since they'd separated. "Maybe your mother would like to come with us." He spoke to Beth while searching Hope's face for the response.

She hesitated, then nodded in uncertain agreement. Spending time with Eric would not be easy. She might enjoy it—too much.

But Hope walked with them to the blue booth with bright green frogs painted all over its walls. It took five dollars and ten darts, but Beth came away from the game a happy little girl with a fat frog tucked under each arm. They'd won an extra one for Cassie.

Then the three of them walked together, with Eric and Beth engaged in conversation. The two were discussing something about school when Hope realized she hadn't been listening closely to what they were saying. She'd been walking along silently, thinking too much about her life with Eric. If the Lord had brought them together, how had they managed to go so far astray?

"You ready to go home, babe?" Eric inquired. Beth nodded her head slowly, as though tired.

"Mom? You ready to go, too?" her daughter asked.

"Yes, hon. I'm ready," Hope replied.

Eric picked Beth up again, and she rested her head on his shoulder as he walked with Hope the short distance to where her red van was parked.

"Daddy? Can't I ride home with you in your truck?" she asked. "Please?"

Eric's black pickup was about a dozen spaces away in the next row over. He looked from the vehicle to Hope. "If it's okay with your mother."

She smiled. "Go ahead. I'll see you at home."

"Okay, Mom. See you later!" Beth responded. Eric reached to open the door of the van for Hope while holding their daughter in his other arm.

Hope moved past him and climbed into the vehicle. Then she slid her key into the ignition.

"Thank you," she said quietly, looking back into Eric's dark gaze.

He nodded without speaking, and closed the door for her. Then he and Beth headed toward the truck. Hope watched them go as she started her van and drove out of the lot.

The "home" Hope was headed toward was the house owned by Ed and Grace Granston, her mother- and father-in-law. They had invited Hope and the girls to stay with them during Cassie's bout with pneumonia. Hope was dividing her time among the necessities: teaching, looking after Beth, and being with eight-year-old Cassie at the hospital every night. Staying with Eric's parents had seemed like the best solution at the time she'd agreed to it. But now, as she neared the two-story white home, she wondered if she'd made the right decision. She'd known she would be around Eric, now and then, if she stayed with his mother and father. But it hadn't happened—until today.

She parked her van in the driveway and turned off the ignition just as Eric pulled in beside her. Hope took a deep breath. "Lord, please help me get through this," she whispered in the silence of her vehicle.

Maybe she and Beth could go upstairs and find something to do. That way, Eric could visit his parents, and Hope could keep her distance from him. She needed to do that, if she was going to let him go. Being near Eric again only reminded her of how much she loved him. And she'd found no provision for dealing with that in the separation agreement she'd refused to sign.

Eric and Beth were halfway to the front steps when Hope got out of her vehicle and walked past Eric's truck. There was a stack of clothes on the seat of the pickup, she noticed. Could he be bringing laundry for his mother to wash? Possibly—but she didn't really think so. It didn't seem like something Eric would do.

Hope walked around the rear of the van. She pulled off her sunglasses and pushed wispy blond bangs from her forehead, just as she saw Beth run into the house ahead of her father. But Eric stopped and waited while Hope walked up the concrete steps to the porch. He held the front door open, glancing in her direction with curiosity. She rarely had been so subdued in their "together" days, she recalled. He was probably wondering why she was so quiet now.

Hope moved past him into the large house. *His* parents' home, she reminded herself. She suddenly felt almost as though she were trespassing. Maybe living here temporarily wasn't such a great idea. Still, even if just for the children's sake, it seemed to be her best option right now. And sometimes, for no explicable reason, it felt to Hope as though the Lord wanted her there.

"I'm sorry, Hope. I haven't even asked how you are," Eric said.

"I'm fine," she replied.

"Did you teach today?"

"No." Hope turned to look at him. She knew that she should attempt to carry on this discussion with him, if only she could think of something neutral they could talk about. And asking about the clothes in the truck didn't seem appropriate. "How's the world of real estate?" she asked.

"It could be better," Eric answered with a slight shrug, "but business will pick up again one of these days. It's nothing for you to worry about."

"I'm not worried," she said quickly. "I was... only trying to make conversation."

One corner of Eric's mouth curved into a half-hearted smile. "That's difficult to do with someone you're accustomed to just talking to."

She nodded in agreement and looked away from him toward their daughter. Eric had always been easy to talk to. That was one of the things she loved about him. That and his gentle nature. And his dark eyes, and the way time had etched featherlike laugh lines at the corners of them.... There were so many things about Eric that she would always love, whether he belonged to her or not. Seeing him again today only reaffirmed what her heart already knew. She was in so deep, she'd probably never get out.

"Beth," she said to her daughter, wanting to change her flow of thought, "If you do your homework and change your clothes, I'll take you over to the hospital to see your sister again before bedtime.''

"Come on, Dad—" the child started up the staircase in a hurry "—you can help me go over my spelling words. I have ten to learn.''

"I'll be there in a minute," he called after Beth as she scampered away from him. Then he and Hope both glanced toward the sound of Ed and Grace Granston's voices coming from the kitchen. Eric returned his gaze to his wife. "Hope...Mom and Dad want to talk to you about something.''

She didn't reply right away; she was too busy noticing the hesitancy she saw in his eyes as he spoke. "It's not about the divorce, is it, Eric? I don't want to sign those papers—"

"It's not," he promised. "You don't have to sign anything you don't want to sign. Just hear them out while I help Beth with her homework.'' Then he turned to go up the stairs toward his daughter's room.

Hope stood silently at the foot of the staircase, remembering her feelings from the night they had parted—her sense of being right. She hadn't realized being "right" could feel so wrong, and she'd missed him almost before he'd walked out the door.

"Hope, dear, is that you?" Grace stuck her head around the kitchen door to see her daughter-in-law standing there, looking at the empty staircase. She adjusted her silver-frame glasses. "Could Ed and I speak with you for a moment?"

Hope followed Grace into the next room. "How are you feeling?" Hope asked her father-in-law when she noticed he looked even paler than he had in recent days.

"Well, that's part of what we want to talk to you about," Grace began. "He's not been feeling as well as he could, and we've decided to take a little vacation for a couple of weeks."

Hope's heart sank. Staying here the past two weeks during Cassie's illness had worked out so well for Hope and Beth that she hadn't given much consideration to the strain it might put on the girls' grandparents. "I'm sorry, Grace. You don't need to leave your own home. Beth and I will find an apartment somewhere close by so you and Ed can—"

"No." Grace and Ed were both shaking their heads in disagreement. "That's just what we *don't* want—you feeling that you need to move out. Ed and I haven't been away from home since that autumn trip to New England over three years ago. It's time for a change of scenery, wouldn't you say? We want you and Beth to stay right here. But while we are away for those two weeks, you'll still need someone around to help when you're at the hospital...so we've asked Eric to move in."

"No," Hope said, shaking her head. "I'll find someone else to help me—"

"If Ed and I are going to relax and enjoy this vacation, we need to know you're here with someone we can count on. That someone is Eric. If you won't let him be the one that stays here in our absence, then we're not going.''

Hope sighed. She needed help from someone, at least during the nights she stayed with Cassie. She knew that. But, Eric? "Grace, let me ask some of the teachers I work with. Maybe one of them could let Beth sleep at their house while you're gone.''

"No," Grace responded flatly. "It's going to be Eric. Cassie and Beth are his children, and this is his responsibility.''

"It would be awkward for us," Hope said as casually as she could manage. *Awkward?* Having Eric around again? Day after day? It would be impossible.

"Call a truce for fourteen days. The arguing can resume once Ed and I come home." Grace glanced toward her silent husband. "Ed, help me out with this.''

"She's right, Hope. As we've said, we *want* you and the girls to stay with us as long as you need to. But you and Eric will have to get along together for a couple of weeks without us. You have children together—you'll have to make this work.''

"But you don't understand what you're asking. Eric and I..." she began and then paused. How could she explain this? "Nothing's been the same since Cassie hurt her back in that dive at the pool.''

"But Cassie recovered beautifully from that injury, thank the Lord," Grace reminded. "She's walking again, and all she needs now is to get over this pneumonia. Soon, she'll be well, she'll be home and life can get back to normal.''

But what was normal? Hope wondered. Life with Eric, or life without him? After all the years of loving him, she wasn't sure anymore.

It was with quiet resignation that she assented to her in-laws' decision. Then she walked slowly up the staircase toward Beth's room. So, that explained the clothes in Eric's truck. He was bringing them here, moving them into a room upstairs. Probably the one across the hall from hers. Hope sighed. She needed help during Ed and Grace's absence. That was true. But she didn't want to need Eric.

"Mom, I'm going back with you to see Cassie again tonight. Right?'' Beth came running out of her room when she heard her mother's footsteps in the hallway. "I've already printed each of my spelling words twice.''

"Good girl,'' Hope said, and gave the child a hug. "Change your clothes, and we'll go.'' Beth ran back into her bedroom to change, out of hearing range, just as Eric stepped out of the room where he had been helping with homework. A sense of inadequacy swept over Hope as she met his serious gaze. Did she really need to accept his help? Couldn't she work this out on her own without relying on this man?

"I have some things to bring in from the truck,'' Eric said. He hesitated, studying her guarded expression before continuing. "Did Mom and Dad talk to you?"

"Yes," she answered. "They told me you're moving in."

"It's the logical thing to do, Hope. No matter how awkward it may be. The girls are my responsibility, too."

Hope nodded her head in agreement, then looked away from Eric. *Responsibility*. Doing what he *should* do. Those were the things that would motivate Eric, and Hope wished it could be more.

Then she looked up at him and asked the question that had nagged at her for days. "Are you angry with me for being here?"

"I'd rather have you and the girls living here with my parents than five hundred miles away in Missouri with yours," he replied quietly. "You know that, don't you?"

"No, I—I guess I just needed to be sure," she answered. *Sure?* She wasn't sure about much of anything involving Eric Granston.

"If you take Beth with you, I'll come by the hospital and pick her up in about an hour," Eric stated. "That way she can have dinner, a bath and get to bed on time."

Hope said simply, "Thank you," and turned toward the guest room she was using during her stay. What an unpleasant two weeks this could turn out to be. Five hundred miles distance between them suddenly sounded good compared to six feet of hallway.

"Come on, hon," Hope said as she gathered up a couple of books from the dresser. "Let's go say good night to Cassie. Dad will pick you up later and bring you home." She took a quick look down the hallway. No Eric in sight.

"Mom, do you have to stay at the hospital every night?" Beth asked with a sigh.

Hope felt torn. She knew it was hard sometimes for Beth, who needed attention and comforting now as much as did her sister. "Maybe not every night," she responded before touching her little girl's soft blond curls, the same shade as her own. "But until she tells me that herself, I'll stay with her. Eight years old is still rather young to be left alone in a hospital. She's nearly well, anyway, and soon she'll be home. Then things will get back to the way you like them."

"And you'll be home more," Beth added.

"Definitely," she agreed, and kissed her daughter on the top of her little blond head. "Then we'll find a new place to live."

"With Dad?"

"No, Beth. Not with Dad." Hope reached for her sweater and purse and glanced at her watch. "Grab your jacket—we've got to go."

"I don't want to move away. I like it here with Grandma and Grandpa," Beth insisted.

Hope nodded. "I know you do. We'll talk about it later. Now, go tell Grandma and Grandpa we're leaving. She's fixing fried chicken for you and Dad to have later."

"Yum! My favorite!" Beth exclaimed as she headed down the staircase away from her mother. She had become more and more independent of Hope since Cassie's accident. Self-preservation, Hope thought a little sadly. In a way, she missed being needed more by her youngest daughter. At least Eric would be around to give Beth more attention. Once again Hope felt herself panic at the thought of sharing the house for two solid weeks. But Cassie was waiting, and it was time to go.

Hope and Beth entered the pastel blue of the hospital room. "Hi, sweetheart. How are you feeling?" Hope gave two children's books and a kiss to her girl.

"Daddy and I won you this!" Beth exclaimed as she placed the friendly looking frog beside her sister. "I have one just like it at home."

"Cool. Thanks, Beth. And I'm doing okay, Mom. I just ate my dinner." Cassie sat up a little straighter in the bed. "I've been watching television."

"I brought the books you asked for. Beth had to help me find them. They were buried in your box of stuffed animals."

"They were way down in the bottom," Beth

added. "Down below Brown Bear, Papa Bear and Bob."

Hope grinned. "Bob" was their oldest teddy bear, and he wore a floppy blue hat and red pants with yellow suspenders. How they had decided on the name, she had no idea, but he'd been "Bob" for as long as anyone could remember.

"Thanks, guys," Cassie said. "I've been missing these books. I'll read one to you tonight, Mom."

"Good," Hope pulled a chair up beside the bed and sat down. "If you feel like it."

"I feel okay. My fever is down—almost gone, Nurse Trudy said."

"Great!" Hope responded. "Maybe, by tomorrow, it will be *all* gone." She knew that Cassie's doctor was reluctant to let her go home—despite her continuing improvement—until he was certain she was well. Completely. The last time she came home after being hospitalized with a lung infection, she suddenly became worse and much to everyone's dismay had to be readmitted. No one wanted that to happen again. "I'll talk to your doctor in the morning. Then I'll find out how you're doing."

"Are you teaching tomorrow?" Cassie asked.

"Yes," Hope answered. "Second grade." She had reduced her workload to substitute teaching after Cassie's diving accident almost two years ago. But Hope taught whenever she could. Since her separation from Eric six months ago, whatever money she earned proved useful. When they had sold their house earlier in the year, they'd split the equity evenly, and Hope was saving her share with the thought of buying a small house of her own when the time was right.

"Guess what?" Beth asked as she climbed up on the bed to sit by Cassie's feet. "Daddy's picking me up in a little while, and we're going home to eat fried chicken with Grandma and Grandpa."

"Lucky you," Cassie remarked.

Her daughter's complexion looked much brighter than it had yesterday, Hope noticed. She leaned forward to touch the girl's cheek. "That sounds good to me, too, hon. We'll have fried chicken to celebrate when you come home, if the doctor says it's okay," Hope added.

And until Cassie came home from the hospital or until her grandparents' vacation ended, Eric would be there, she reminded herself. How could Hope explain to the girls that he would be living with them again, and yet not let them expect too much? Especially, when she was having difficulty keeping her own wants and wishes in line.

"Cassie, Beth. Do you know Grandma and Grandpa are going to be gone for a while? They're taking a little vacation."

"Grandma told me they're going on a cruise," Cassie confirmed. "She's always wanted to do that. She told me this morning."

Hope nodded her head. "Right, well, while they

are gone, they think I need someone to help out around the house.''

"Like a housekeeper? Like some of the families on TV have?'' Beth asked.

"No,'' Hope answered, suddenly feeling thankful that her life wasn't as mixed up as some of the sitcoms she'd seen. "No, they asked your father to move in while they're away. So...Dad will be living there. With us. Temporarily.''

The girls' faces lit up like fireworks. Just the response Hope had feared.

"Yeah! Dad's coming home! When?'' Beth squealed. Cassie was a little more reserved, smiling broadly, but not asking any questions.

"He's moving some of his clothes and belongings from his apartment—''

"I never did like that apartment he had over the office, anyway,'' Cassie remarked. "I'd rather have him at Grandma's with us.''

"Me, too!'' Beth chimed in.

"But, remember, it's only for a short period of time,'' Hope reminded. "Just a couple of weeks or less.''

"Or more,'' Beth replied.

"No,'' Hope stated firmly, and gathered Beth into her arms. "This is just for a little while.''

"But this is exactly what we were praying for, isn't it, Cassie? Ever since Dad left—''

"Beth, honey, Dad and I aren't getting back together. We're just going to be staying in the same house for a while," Hope explained as a sudden pang of loneliness hit her. How she wished it did mean more. She and Eric had known many happy years together.

Beth still sounded optimistic. "Maybe he'll start going to church again. Wouldn't that be good? He could teach Sunday School like he used to do. I know the kids miss him. And he could be trusted again."

"You mean a 'trustee,'" Cassie corrected.

A flash of humor crossed Hope's face. Then it was gone. Maybe Beth was right. Hope had stopped trusting him. Lord knows, Eric had given her enough reason to do so.

"Girls, this is exactly what I was afraid of. Don't get excited over this. Nothing has changed between your father and me."

"But prayer changes things," Cassie said with sincerity. "You said so yourself."

"Yes, it can change things," Hope responded, "but God doesn't answer every prayer with a 'yes.'"

"But some of them, He does," Beth argued.

Some of them, He does. Hope couldn't argue with that. She'd seen many prayers answered in her lifetime, one of the greatest being Cassie's complete recovery from serious injuries she'd sustained at a pool two summers ago. The girl had regained her ability to walk again and returned to a normal life, although it had taken time and therapy. Too much of both, according to Eric. And that was only part of what had driven him away from the Lord, from church and from his family.

But through it all, he had never blamed Hope. Not for anything. Sometimes she wondered if she'd have felt less guilty if he had.

"Hi, girls. How ya doin'?"

Eric's voice sounded pleasant, almost soothing as he greeted the children. Hope glanced up from fluffing Cassie's pillow to see him enter the room with a smile. A nice smile. The kind she could almost believe was meant for her.

"Ready for some chicken? I'm starving," Beth said as she picked up her pink jacket and ran to give her big sister a hug.

"'Bye, Beth. Save some of that food for me!" Cassie called as Beth headed toward the door.

Eric kissed Cassie and mussed up her hair a little before he walked away. "I'll see you again tomorrow, sweetie." Then he looked directly at Hope. "I'd be glad to stay here if you're tired. You could use a good night's rest at home, you know."

Home. Exactly where was that? It used to be wherever Eric was. She shook her head. "Thanks, anyway, but I'm fine tonight. Maybe some other time."

Eric nodded in reluctant agreement. "Then, we'll see you in the morning," he responded quietly.

Hope saw a flicker of uncertainty, almost a tenderness, in Eric's gaze before he took Beth's hand and turned to go. His dark brown hair was cut short and silky straight in complete contrast to the blond curls of the little girl who gazed up at him as they walked away. Eric hadn't changed his clothes since she'd seen him earlier. His gray slacks and white shirt were slightly rumpled, and his dark blue tie was loosened but still present. He had that weary look about him that Hope wanted to soothe away with the right words or a soft touch. She lowered her clear blue gaze to the pillow she still held in her hands. She missed him. Deeply. She didn't want to, but she did.

"Mom, ready for me to read to you?"

She returned her gaze and attention to her bright-eyed daughter. "Of course, I am, hon. Just let me move these cushions around and turn this cot into a bed." Hope picked up the extra folded blanket she had brought from home so she could make herself comfortable on the makeshift bed. Nights of unsettled sleep sometimes brought an achiness into Hope's shoulders that she couldn't quite overcome, and she knew she would miss Grace's occasional backrubs. They'd been almost as good as the ones Eric had given over the years. No, on second thought, Hope considered as she remembered her husband's strong, warm touch, they weren't *that* good.

"Cassie, hon," she said, wanting to think of

something else—anything else—but Eric, "I think it's time for you to read."

As Eric led Beth through the maze of hospital corridors and out to the parking lot, he was thoughtful. He wanted to help Hope in whatever ways she would allow, and he knew there might not be many. He'd avoided her for too long, but only in an attempt to protect his own heart. Maybe she wouldn't forgive him. Maybe he was too late. And maybe asking his parents to go away on an unscheduled vacation wouldn't prove to be the perfect solution he hoped it might be. He guessed the next two weeks would give him the answers he needed.

Chapter Two

"C'mon, Carrie Elizabeth. We're gonna be late," Hope said, grabbing the car keys early the next morning. She had returned to the house to pick Beth up for school. "Let's go."

"If you're in a hurry to leave, I can take her to school," Eric offered as he entered the kitchen. Streams of sunshine through the window lit up the room. "I have a few extra minutes this morning."

"You're sure?" she asked hesitantly. Having Eric walk through a doorway at any moment was something she had to get used to. And, could, too easily.

"I'm sure," he answered, reaching for Beth as she ran into the room directly toward her father. "'Mornin', babe."

"Dad! You really are still here!"

"That, I am." Eric hugged her small frame to him, then released her. "Your grandparents must be sleeping late. C'mon, let's eat a quick breakfast so you can make it to school on time."

He glanced up at Hope, surprised to see her still standing there in the doorway, watching them. "If you see Cassie before I do this afternoon, tell her I'll be there later today," he said, looking into her fathomless blue eyes a moment longer than he should have.

"Give me a kiss, honey. I'll see you at school later." She kissed her daughter, then glanced at Eric again. "Thank you. I need to get there early to look over the lesson plans," she said before leaving through the back door.

Eric's presence, his helpfulness and kindness, could be difficult to accept, she knew, but it could also be the Lord's way of showing them His will for their lives…something Hope hadn't felt very certain of lately. For years she'd believed that she was following the right course, living in the center of God's will, and that the love He'd blessed Eric and her with would go on forever. She'd given her heart to the Lord at the conclusion of a Sunday School class one day when she was only six years old. The teacher had asked if anyone wanted to pray for salvation, and Hope had raised her hand. So her heart had belonged to God even before it belonged to Eric Granston.

She climbed into her van and started toward

Beechmore Elementary, still lost in thought. Eric was now with her again, but only because he didn't think she was capable of handling everything by herself while Ed and Grace were away. And he was probably right, she lamented. She needed his help to get Beth to school on time and to be there with her at night while Hope slept at the hospital. She stopped for a red light. Yes, he was being helpful and considerate, almost friendly. But where was the Eric she'd married and loved? He certainly wasn't the man who was at this moment sharing breakfast with their six-year-old daughter. The Eric she used to know would have kissed her good morning, said a prayer over their breakfast and shared a cup of coffee with her.

The blaring horn of the automobile behind her returned Hope's attention to the traffic light, which had changed to green. She continued on her way as her thoughts went in another direction. Eric wasn't the only one who'd changed since Cassie's accident, she realized. She'd never kept secrets from him before, not until that summer day at the pool.

Entering the familiar school parking lot, she carefully pulled into the first available space. She'd been convinced years ago that the Lord had brought Eric into her life. And He had blessed their union in many ways. Could He have done all that—given them such happiness for so many years—only to let them mess things up like this? Now that Cassie was better and life held such promise? Hope didn't have all the answers, but somehow, some way, there had to be more in her future with Eric Granston than a divorce decree—if only they could find their way to it.

"How did you meet Mom?" Cassie asked between bites of cherry-red gelatin from her lunch tray later that day. Eric had finished up earlier than expected at a closing and had stopped in to see how his daughter was feeling.

He leaned back in his chair. *Meet her?* He could barely remember a time when he hadn't known Hope Ryan Granston. "We met in kindergarten, I guess. We went through school together, graduated from high school and then college together."

Cassie grinned from ear to ear. "So you were childhood sweethearts?"

"Yes, you could say that," he responded quietly, reflecting on earlier days. "We were friends for a long time before it became a boyfriend/girlfriend relationship during high school. Your mother was very popular in school, you know. She was pretty and smart, and fun to be with."

"Don't you think she's all those things anymore, Dad?"

"Yes, I do." He answered her question before his mind went back, momentarily, to envision the teenager he had fallen in love with. Hope's blond hair had been short then, in an almost boyish cut, but the style had looked good on her. She was thin and athletic, an excellent student and a sports fan.

"So, it wasn't like they say in the movies? Love at first sight?"

Eric smiled. "You're very nosy today," he remarked. "But I guess with your mother and me, it was more like friendship at first sight. The love part kind of caught us by surprise." Very much by surprise, he recalled as he thought of that long walk home from the high school one day.

It was years ago. Several inches of snow had fallen during the afternoon. After school, he and Hope had trudged through the fresh snow, both of them loaded down with books and gym bags. Eric was carrying Hope's clarinet case. They were cutting across the field that adjoined the property owned by Hope's parents when Eric tripped over something in his path, falling facedown in the snow. The books flew to one side and the gym bag and clarinet case to the other as he hit the ground hard. And although the fall hurt his shoulder a little bit, nothing hurt as badly as his fourteen-year-old pride.

But Hope hadn't laughed. She certainly could have been amused by the sight of him clumsily plunging into the white depths. But she hadn't. "Eric!" Hope had called out his name, in a typically feminine, almost maternal, manner. "Are you all right? Did you hurt yourself?" She dropped her belongings on the ground and knelt beside him as he sat up, slightly stunned by the incident.

Eric wiped snow from his face. "I'm okay—just embarrassed," he replied, as Hope pulled off her red gloves and brushed more snow from his face with warm hands.

"There's nothing to be embarrassed about," she'd responded, pushing strands of hair away from her friend's forehead in a tender touch. Friends. That's all they were, wasn't it? In that moment, it didn't feel that way to Eric. Hope knelt only inches from him in that field, with her jeans getting wet from the snow, while she looked for a long moment into the dark eyes that viewed her with new interest. "A fall like that—" she hesitated before lowering her luminous blue gaze to look away from him "—could happen...to anyone." She stumbled through the sentence. Then, she cautiously looked back at him to find that his eyes hadn't strayed from her face. She smiled a little, and Eric thought for the first time how beautiful she was. Awash in unfamiliar thoughts, he slowly leaned forward, his mouth brushing hers in a soft kiss that she returned, tentatively at first, then, gradually, with a little more confidence. They finally broke apart abruptly, each of them settling back into the snow and gasping for breath—

"Dad," Cassie interrupted the private memory, "tell me about how you fell in love."

The straight line of Eric's mouth showed no hint

of the emotion behind his memories. "It's difficult to tell anyone about the precise moment you know you're in love, Cass. You'll understand that when you're older." But in fact, Eric knew exactly when it had been for him: that afternoon in the snow. During that warm kiss that caused him to forget about his fall, his sore shoulder and the books lying where they had dropped. After that kiss, Eric and Hope had belonged to each other.

He cleared his throat. "Did you know your mother was the only girl on the high school golf team in those days? There wasn't a girls' team yet, and she played well enough that she was invited to join the boys." He laughed quietly at the memory he always had whenever he thought about her golfing days—Hope surrounded by males.

"Weren't you jealous?" Cassie asked as she took another bite of the meal she'd been picking at. It was as though she could read his mind. "Mom being around all those other guys?"

"You bet I was. I didn't like it at all, and I wasn't a good enough golfer to make the team, so she was on her own." Just like now, he thought briefly.

"What if she gets married again someday? It won't matter to you?"

"Married? You don't need to worry about that happening soon," Eric remarked, wanting to bring an end to this topic. Unless Cassie knew something he didn't. He hadn't been around enough lately to be aware of what was going on in Hope's life, but his daughter was usually good at telling everything she knew about a subject without being prodded. So, he waited.

Cassie coughed several times. "Well, maybe not real soon, I guess."

"What does that mean?" Eric asked. He reached for a nearby pitcher of water and poured some of it into the plastic cup on her lunch tray.

"Nothing. It's just that Mr. Shelton, the principal, has been talking to her about the future, and they have eaten lunch together at school. Does that count as anything?" she asked in between sips.

It counted. But Eric wouldn't let any emotion register there in front of his daughter. Not even surprise, and that wasn't all he was feeling.

"Dad, you didn't answer me."

"Lunch in a school cafeteria with dozens of other people wouldn't be much of a date now, would it?" Eric said.

"I guess not," she replied.

But it was enough to bother Eric. *Shelton.* He didn't recall anyone by that name at Cassie's school, and he'd been there quite a few times. "I thought you had a female principal. Mrs. White, wasn't it?"

"That was *last* year, Dad. Mrs. White had a baby, and she wanted to take some time off."

"So Mr. Shelton replaced Mrs. White?"

"Yes, and he's a—what's the word? His wife died, and he's a—"

"Widower?" Eric finished.

"Yes, that's it. He has a son and a daughter, younger than me. Grandma says he needs a wife. I heard her and Mom talking about it."

Eric watched Cassie push her food away, only half-eaten. "Why don't you at least eat that applesauce, Cass. You love applesauce."

"I *used* to love it. Now, it tastes *gross*."

Something else he hadn't known. Suddenly, Eric felt very alone. He wasn't around enough to keep up with the changes that were happening with his children—or with Hope, apparently. Was she really interested in this Shelton guy who supposedly "needed" a wife? Or could it possibly be some kind of potential "arrangement"? No, she would never settle for something like that. Not Hope. Not after having known how good a real marriage could be. He glanced out the window. And theirs had been good, for a very long time.

"Dad, what's wrong?" Cassie's question drew his attention back to her, and he studied her pretty blue eyes so similar in color to her mother's.

"Nothing, hon. What were we talking about earlier? Mom being on the golf team, wasn't it?"

"Yeah," Cassie replied. "I wonder if those boys teased her about being the only girl?"

"In the beginning they did. But then she hit a three wood two hundred yards down the fairway to help them win a championship. That brought an end to the teasing." Eric thought of the strong-willed attitude his wife often displayed. Hope wouldn't have stopped playing on that team even if the teasing had continued. If she wanted something, she went after it. At least, she used to. Surely, life hadn't changed her so much that she'd consider a relationship of convenience with a widower she barely knew. Had it?

"Can't you and Mom stop being mad at each other? I know it was all because of me that you—"

"Cassie," Eric gently interrupted her. "You know we've talked about this before. And your mom has talked about it with you, too. The problems between your mother and me have nothing to do with you. And we're not really mad at each other. Not anymore." At least, he wasn't. But he knew it might take a little time to learn Hope's feelings.

"Finished with your lunch?" a nurse asked as she entered the room. "How are you doin' today, Mr. Granston?" she added when she noticed Eric sitting in the chair beside the bed.

"Fine, Trudy. Thanks," Eric answered while watching her take away Cassie's plate, still half-full of her noon meal. The dinner roll and the gelatin were all that had interested her.

"Now, look here, Cassie. You're going to have to do better eating these meals or I'll have to come in here and feed you. You got that?" Trudy threatened with a friendly grin.

"Are you going to be here tonight?" Cassie asked. "I like it best when you're here."

"I'll be here for sure, hon. I'm working a double shift today. Now, you lie down and rest for a while. I'll be back to check your temperature." Then she turned to Eric. "Mr. Granston, why don't you go on down to the cafeteria? I'll keep an eye on your daughter for you for a while."

Eric stood up and stretched his long legs. "I could use a sandwich and a cup of coffee. Cassie, maybe you can get to sleep if I'm not in here talking to you." He ran a hand through his dark hair before leaning down to kiss Cassie. "I'll be back in about twenty minutes, princess."

Then he slipped out the door, stepped into an empty elevator and pushed the button for the lobby. Happy memories of wintry days and warm kisses in the snow had momentarily taken the edge off reality. He'd lost Hope, and getting her back was going to be difficult. If not impossible.

The elevator stopped, the doors came open and Eric came face to face with the very object of his thoughts.

"Hello," he said and stepped out.

"Hi. I didn't realize you were coming here," Hope replied, looking startled to see him.

"This morning's closing finished quickly, so I stopped by," Eric replied. "Where's Beth?"

"She's still at school," Hope answered as she

tucked some hair behind an ear. "I only had to teach until noon today."

Eric nodded. Then there was awkward silence between them. Now what? Eric wondered. *Lunch,* he suddenly remembered. "I'm going to get some lunch. Cassie is finished eating, and she's resting right now."

"Oh, well, maybe I'll wait a while before I go up." Hope readjusted the slipping shoulder strap of her canvas tote bag before it could slide down her arm. "She won't rest at all if I walk in right now."

"That's probably true," Eric said. "I'm on my way to the cafeteria for something to eat. Want to come along?"

Hope looked at him in what she knew was probably an amusing combination of surprise and skepticism. She couldn't quite believe he was making the offer.

"You can go on up if you'd rather. I won't be offended," he added, then paused.

Hope smiled. "Actually, I'd like to talk to you about something. Maybe this would be a good time."

Oh, no, Eric thought, what did she want to discuss? Did it involve a guy named Shelton? He pointed toward the nearby cafeteria. "Let's go," he said, and they walked down the hallway together in an uncomfortable silence until they entered the à la carte line.

"Coffee, please," Eric requested of the waitress

behind the counter. Then he ordered the special of the day: grilled cheese with a bowl of tomato soup, and coffee. Hope asked for the same, but with decaf instead of regular coffee.

Soon they were seated at one end of a long cafeteria table, eating together for the first time in months. "I don't know, but I'm wondering if maybe we should have ordered something else," Hope remarked after sampling a bite of her sandwich. "Grilled cheese in a restaurant is hardly ever as good as homemade."

Eric watched a frown crease her forehead. "You're probably right. But it looked better than the other choices."

"That's true," Hope replied with a brief smile. "Maybe we should have chosen another place to eat." Then her smile faded. Maybe she shouldn't have said something that hinted at more than he'd offered. She hadn't thought how it might sound until the words were out.

"Maybe so," Eric agreed, easing the moment of tension he'd seen on her face. "You wanted to talk to me?" he asked. His curiosity was increasing.

"Yes," she agreed, "I do need to discuss something about Beth with you."

"She's not sick—"

"No, no, Eric, it's nothing like that. I didn't mean to scare you," Hope responded. "It's just that, she's becoming something of a discipline problem at school. I've been with Cassie so much lately, I didn't notice Beth's behavior. When I picked her up at school the other day, Greg Shelton, the principal, took me aside and filled me in on some facts I wasn't aware of.''

Eric took a sip of his coffee. ''And did Greg have some ideas on how to solve the problems?'' Like spend the rest of your life with him, maybe? he thought unkindly.

Hope frowned in response to his question. ''Do you know him?''

''No,'' Eric said with a shake of his head. ''But I've heard about him.'' And about his needs as perceived by Grandma, Eric thought. ''So, what did he tell you?''

''Beth has been sent to his office twice this month.''

''For what?''

''At first, she was repeatedly talking when she wasn't supposed to, then she was disrespectful to another child. But then it progressed quickly to intentional disobedience when she started refusing to do what her teacher told her to do. She lost her recess every day last week without telling me, and the notes her teacher has sent home to me—Beth's destroyed them! Greg is really worried about what this is going to turn into if we don't take some action. Soon. And so am I.''

''I'll talk to her,'' Eric assured her. ''But Beth is good at hiding her feelings, so it might not be easy to get to the bottom of this matter, even though I think we both know the root of it.''

''Her sister's illness,'' Hope said. ''But Beth is more like you in temperament than she's ever been like me. I'm hoping you can help her in some way I can't.'' Hope looked down at what remained of her lunch as she gathered her thoughts. ''Grace told me about her plans for the cruise when I saw her a little while ago. She said they're leaving tonight for Florida.'' She looked up. Now for the difficult part. ''I appreciate your willingness to stay with us while they're gone.''

Eric stared into the gentle blue eyes that seemed even prettier now than in the years that had passed. ''You don't mind my being there?'' he asked.

''Eric, it's not easy for me to admit this, but I really need your help,'' Hope replied.

He nodded. It wasn't the answer he'd wanted, but it was an acceptable one—a place to begin. ''I'll do what I can, Hope. You know that.''

''I know, but…I must be doing something wrong with Beth. She seems to want to be independent of me, and yet, honestly, I think she needs more of me than she gets.'' Hope blinked hard, and Eric knew she was fighting back tears. ''Being here for Cassie, substitute teaching and taking care of the basics at your parents' home is about all I can deal with these days, Eric. Beth turning into a disciplinary problem wasn't something I'd thought would ever happen, but it has. And, I feel like I'm not doing a good job as a mother.''

"You're exactly the mother she needs, Hope," Eric stated quietly. He knew how hard she could be on herself. "But if she needs extra attention right now, then I'll be there for her."

Hope wiped her mouth on her paper napkin. "Just spend time with her, maybe help with her homework like you did yesterday, watch her play ball...anything like that would mean a lot." She studied Eric's face without smiling, and wondered how he could have stopped loving her. After all they'd shared together? Then she realized she'd been silent too long. "I—I want to thank you."

"You don't need to thank me for helping out with my own children—" he began.

"No," she interrupted. "I mean, I really want to thank you. Since our separation, you've not neglected the girls at all. I was afraid that—" She stopped, knowing she might be entering territory better left alone.

"You were afraid that what? I'd not want to see my kids?" Eric prodded, his instinctive defenses kicking in.

"I don't know," she admitted. "Maybe I thought your new life-style would occupy too much of your time to allow room for the girls. I was very wrong."

"You were," he stated with a hint of a smile. "And thanks. It's generous of you to admit it." His words were spoken gently and prompted no more than a slight smile from Hope.

"Maybe we should go up to see if Cassie's sleeping," she suggested.

"Okay," Eric agreed. "I've had about all of this grilled cheese I can handle anyway."

"It definitely looked better than it tasted," Hope commented as they both carried their trays to the trash can.

A walk through the lobby and an elevator ride up to the fourth floor were all that stood between them and their daughter. Soon they were back in her room where they found Cassie sleeping soundly.

Nurse Trudy appeared at the door. "She's doing fine today. No fever at all."

Hope nodded. "That's great. Thanks, Trudy."

"No problem, Mrs. Granston. I just like to keep the parents informed how the little ones are doing. Did you enjoy your lunch?" she asked, glancing toward Eric with a questioning look.

"The coffee was much better than the food," he responded, laughing. Then he turned to Hope. "If you need me, try calling the office."

"I will," replied Hope. Eric leaned down to kiss Cassie's forehead, then left for the real estate office to finish up the day's business. He entered the hospital parking lot and he quickly located his truck. He'd have to find a way to work this out with Hope, he thought. And he'd have to do so on his own, he knew. After all, he hadn't allowed God into his life for a very long time.

Some days, though, the idea of having a Heavenly Father to turn to again sounded good. Very good.

"It isn't my fault if the teacher isn't fair to me," Beth complained. "She just doesn't like me."

Eric repositioned his arm around Beth as they sat at the head of her bed, talking. Discussing the discipline issues with her was going as Eric had thought it would. Not easily. Beth snuggled up close to him, and he kissed the top of her blond curls. "Mrs. Lindstrom likes you very much, Beth, and I've heard you talk about what a great teacher she is."

"But now it's different."

"How?" he asked.

"Just different. You know, because Cassie is sick again," Beth replied, fidgeting with the blue-satin bow on the teddy bear that sat next to her on the bed. "Do you think I'm too old to keep Brown Bear around?" she asked as she gave the stuffed animal a fierce hug.

"No, not if you still want him, sweetheart." Eric sat quietly, pondering what he should say next. The problem seemed to be less about what was taking place at school than what was taking place in the rest of Beth's life. "Honey, Cassie is sick again, that's true. But it shouldn't change how you feel about your teacher, how your teacher feels about you...or your behavior in the classroom."

"But it's just that—Cassie was Mrs. Lindstrom's favorite student *ever,*" Beth emphasized. "I might as well not exist."

"But Mrs. Lindstrom has kept you after school to go for ice cream, you've been to her apartment to meet her husband and see their aquarium. She hasn't spent time with all the children like that, has she?"

"I don't know," Beth answered. "I just know it's 'Cassie, this' and 'Cassie, that.' 'How is your sister feeling, Beth? Will she be coming home soon? Tell us how she's doing today.' Cassie, Cassie, Cassie!" She burst into tears and buried her face in her father's side.

Eric's arms closed around her a little more tightly. "And it makes you angry because sometimes you want it to be Beth she asks about." He spoke softly, and she nodded her head while continuing to sob. He sighed. "Mrs. Lindstrom may really be trying to make you feel important by letting you share with the class about your sister's hospital experiences. It doesn't mean she loves Cassie more than she loves you, honey."

"Oh, yes, it does!" Beth cried. "Stuff about Cassie is always more important than stuff about me. Always!"

How was he going to help her find her way through this situation? Maybe he needed a different approach. "It's hard being the youngest kid in the family, isn't it?" he remarked. This was something he could identify with. "I was the youngest in my family, too, only I had a sister *and* a brother older than me. Sometimes that wasn't any fun at all."

Beth's crying began to ease a bit, and she raised her head to study her father's face through eyes reddened from rubbing. Then the hiccups started; they quite often followed one of her crying spells. Eric smiled as he thought of Hope. Sometimes, the same thing happened with her.

"Really? You were—the—youngest?" Beth hiccuped.

Eric nodded. "Still am. Always will be," he added. "Of course, neither one of them was seriously ill when we were growing up, so it's not quite the same as your relationship with Cassie."

"But, did some of the teachers like Uncle Rob or Aunt Angela better?"

"Yes," he answered. "My brother and sister were both better students than I was. And much less of a discipline problem, too."

"You mean, you got into more trouble?"

"Sure did. I'd hate to think how many times your grandmother was called to school over something I'd done."

Beth laughed between hiccups. "Did she spank you?"

"Sometimes. But as I got older, the punishment changed to being grounded."

"Like not being allowed to have a friend over to play?"

"Yes, something like that. You see, Rob and Angela were the ones the teachers always liked. By the time I came along, they'd already assumed I was going to be a problem."

"Did that make you mad?"

Eric shrugged. "Kind of, I guess. But I got used to it over the years. Then, one day, a teacher I really liked—"

"What was her name?"

"Mrs. Flowers." Eric could still picture that dark-haired older teacher in his mind. "I accused her of liking Rob and Angela better, and she informed me that wasn't true at all. That she'd always liked me the best, and if I felt that she didn't like me, that was my own fault for thinking that way. Sometimes we set ourselves up for disappointment by *expecting* disappointment."

"Since you thought the teacher liked them more than she liked you, you felt real bad. Even if she didn't really like them one bit better."

He nodded his head and squeezed his little girl affectionately. "Exactly. You're as special and unique as Cassie is. It's just that, since she's sick, she gets the most attention sometimes. Not just from Mom or me, but from teachers and neighbors and friends, too. None of that means you are loved any less than your sister."

Beth's young face clouded over again as more

tears rose to the surface. "I love Cassie so much, Daddy, but sometimes...I just get so *mad* at her."

Eric reached for a couple of tissues and tenderly wiped some trickling tears away. "Because sometimes she seems like the only important person around here?"

Beth nodded and melted into her father's embrace as the sobbing returned. "She is, sometimes, isn't she? Because she got hurt and sick and stuff?"

"No," Eric said emphatically. "She's never more important than you, hon. Never. It's just that, sometimes she needs us more at the moment than you do. I know all of this is difficult for you to sort out because you're so young, but your mother and I love you just as much as we love Cassie. Every bit as much. We always will."

"Even when I get so mad at her? She can't help that she's sick and everybody asks about her."

"It's okay to feel that way sometimes. Everyone does," he explained.

Just then, Eric heard a noise. Glancing up, he saw Hope standing in the doorway with windblown hair and her jacket still on, having just returned from the hospital. She sent Eric a slight frown and a worried look, but he shook his head. He mouthed the words "She's okay" to relieve her concern.

"If Cassie dies, I'll never forgive her," Beth blurted out between sobs, surprising both of her parents with her words. "Never!"

Eric hugged her snugly against him and rocked

back and forth in a soothing motion, wanting to calm her fears. "Cassie's nearly well, honey. She'll be home soon, and things will be back to normal. She's not leaving us."

"But I want her home *now*. Nothing's the same without her. There's a place in my heart where she fits," Beth said.

Hope's hand flew to cover her mouth and silence the cry that threatened to slip out, and Eric's eyes stung with hot, unshed tears. He kissed the top of Beth's head and cleared his throat roughly before he could speak again. "Beth, sweetheart, it'll be okay. I promise."

Hope blinked several times, fighting the tears welling up in her own eyes. Then she entered the room. "Beth?"

The little girl raised her head to see Hope smiling at her. "Mom," was all she said as she moved from her father's arms into her mother's. Their fierce, clinging hug left Eric with an odd twinge of emptiness. Beth loved him deeply—he knew that. But for the girls, at times, there was no place like the comfort of Hope's arms. Eric understood that. Sometimes, he felt that way, too.

"You okay?" Hope asked in a whisper against Beth's soft hair as she closed her eyes and held her daughter close to her heart.

"Yes," Beth answered. "Daddy and I were just talking about Cassie and Mrs. Lindstrom and stuff."

"'Stuff,' huh?" Hope teased. "Sounds important."

"Very," Eric commented. He stood up, suddenly feeling out of place. "But now that you're here—"

"No, Daddy. Don't go. Stay with us for a while," Beth pleaded. "He doesn't have to go, does he, Mom?"

"No, he doesn't have to go." She turned her gaze to Eric. "Maybe he could come downstairs with us and have some hot chocolate. Okay?" she added.

"Okay, Mom."

Hope allowed Beth to slide out of her arms, and they started toward the stairs.

"Marshmallows?" Hope asked as she rummaged through a kitchen cabinet. "Where would Grandma keep the marshmallows?"

"Right beside the honey on the top shelf. See it, up high?" Beth was pointing to the package.

"Ah, yes, I do," Hope responded, stretching to try to grab the cellophane bag.

Eric reached past her, easily retrieved it, then placed it on the counter in front of her.

"Thank you," she said.

"You're welcome," he answered, reaching for cups in the cupboard above the sink. He glanced over at her, wondering if she would drink hot chocolate with them. She had always been the healthy eater in the family, avoiding too much of anything—including chocolate and milk. But he didn't need to ask. Hope had guessed his question.

"Yes, I'll have some, too," she said with a playful smile. "I'm not the picky eater I used to be. I've changed some over the last year."

"We probably both have," Eric remarked. But he lost his train of thought while studying her delicately carved features and those pretty eyes of cornflower blue. Being around Hope, he knew, wouldn't be easy. That's why he'd avoided her for much too long. Because of difficult moments just like this when her mouth curved into one of those gentle smiles he remembered so well. Being near her and not touching her was quite a balancing act. He placed three mugs on the counter and moved away from her to join Beth at the table. "Did Cassie feel better tonight?" he asked to break the silence.

"Yes," Hope responded. "She really had a lot more energy." Hope poured milk into the cups and placed them in Grace's microwave. "Believe it or not, she asked if she could stay alone tonight—first time ever. I told her I'd come home to see Beth, then go back over to the hospital to say good-night and to see if she'd changed her mind."

She reached out to tug on a lock of her daughter's light hair, prompting a halfhearted complaint. "Mom! Stop!"

"All right," Hope replied. "You really should be asleep, you know? Maybe Dad will tuck you in tonight." Hope raised her eyes to meet Eric's gaze—a gaze that seemed to linger on her. "That way I can get back over to the hospital quicker."

"You stay home with Beth," he offered. "I'll go back to the hospital to check on Cass."

Hope's expression looked...grateful, he finally decided. She was probably relieved at the thought of enjoying the luxury of a good night's rest. Not that it was anyone's fault but Hope's that she was staying at the hospital too much. Eric stayed whenever Hope agreed to it, which was seldom.

"Thank you," she said quietly. "I could use the time here at home." Then she looked away from Eric and into the cups she had retrieved from the microwave. She then added chocolate to the milk. *Home.* That word kept popping up in her mind. Why? Probably because Eric was around so much. She set a cup in front of each of them and joined them at the table. Staying here with Ed and Grace could not last long. No, she knew that was out of the question. Ed's health wasn't good enough for them to stay here indefinitely. And these were Eric's parents, not her own—although there were times she nearly forgot that fact. Sometimes she almost wished she didn't love them quite so much, didn't feel as comfortable as she always did in their company. Eric's family had become *her* family over the years. And that would be difficult to let go of.

"Hope? Are you okay?" Eric asked, his words

suddenly cutting through her thoughts and returning her to the present.

"Yes, sorry. I guess I let my mind wander. What were you saying?" She met Eric's eyes, dark with concern.

"I was asking if the doctor said he might release Cassie soon?"

"Yes, this morning he said that she might get out in a couple of days." She took a sip of her drink and silently wished she had added a few marshmallows to her own cup. "Beth, would you hand that bag to me?"

Beth complied, and Eric watched in obvious amusement as Hope added a handful of the white fluffy sweetness to her cocoa.

"There couldn't be much nutritional value in there, Hope," he remarked to the wife who throughout their marriage had preached the hazards of too much sugar.

Hope shrugged. "The hot chocolate in the vending machines at the hospital has marshmallows in it, and I've gotten used to it. Hot chocolate doesn't taste right without them now." Kind of like life without Eric, she mused.

Eric excused himself from the table and stood up, delivering his empty cup to the sink. He kissed Beth on the temple. "I'm going to the hospital to see my other little blondie," he said with a smile that faded as he looked from Beth to Hope. He saw the weariness in her eyes, and it worried him more than he'd say. "Get some rest, hon—" he began, then stopped. But it was too late. He turned his head to look away from the awkward surprise he'd glimpsed in her wide-eyed expression. The mistake had surprised him, too. "'Hope,' I mean," he corrected, trying to bring a quick end to the embarrassing moment. "I'll be back in a little while."

"Thank you," she said, and nothing else. But one corner of her mouth tipped up into a half smile as she watched him leave. "And thank you, Lord," she whispered. Maybe things weren't as hopeless as they sometimes seemed.

Eric shook his head in frustration after he walked out of the room. How could he let a term of endearment like that slip out so easily? But he already knew the answer. He still thought of her in that way—that's how. Eric grabbed a jacket from the coatrack near the door, and stepped out into the chilly night air. She was the mother of his children, the best friend he'd ever had...and the woman he loved and wanted. They'd been happy before; all they needed was the chance to begin again. They both deserved to be happy, didn't they? Surely, God wouldn't deny them that. Eric glanced up at the black sky as though he could see straight through to God Himself. No, Eric corrected himself, he would never again speculate on what God would or wouldn't do. He'd seen where that had taken him once before in life. Once was enough.

* * *

"Hi, princess," Eric greeted Cassie as he entered the familiar hospital room. He gently grabbed a small foot through the soft yellow blanket covering her legs.

"Dad, hi!" Her face lit up when she saw him, and nothing pleased him more.

"So you want to spend a night by yourself, huh?" he asked, pulling her into a brief, but warm embrace. Then he reached for the old green chair he'd grown accustomed to sitting in during this hospital stay.

"Isn't Trudy here now? I can't believe you want to stay all night alone if your favorite nurse isn't on duty."

"She's here. She just went to get me some cookies and juice for a bedtime snack. Go home, Dad. I'm ready to try it alone." Cassie's smile had a guilty edge to it.

"What's up with you?" he asked.

"It will be good for you and Mom to both be home tonight. Together. In the same house. Don't you think?" She giggled.

"So, that's the motive," he responded, grabbing her foot and tickling it while she laughed. "I knew there was something going on in that smart little brain of yours. You think your mother and I need help with our relationship?"

"Dad, I think you need all the help you can get."

Then it was Eric's turn to laugh. Mostly in surprise. "Thanks a lot for your confidence in dear old

Dad,'' he remarked, then took more serious note of what Cassie was implying. "I can't promise things will work out with us. Be patient. We'll see how it goes."

"Do you still love Mom?"

"Yes, Cassie. I'll always love your mother." He leaned forward to kiss her forehead. "Always."

Now, all he needed was a way to prove it—to the girls, and to Hope.

Chapter Three

❧

"How can you let them treat you that way, Hope?" Eric's words had been quiet, but firm. He'd returned home to find Hope in the middle of a long-distance telephone conversation with her mother. And he hadn't liked the part he'd overheard. "You deserve better than that."

"You handle your parents your way, and I'll handle mine my way," Hope replied. Discussing her relationship with her parents was never easy with Eric. He always defended her too much, sided with her more than she felt he should. Didn't he understand her motivation for any of this?

Eric studied her determined expression. Her sapphire eyes were as fiery as her temper, and she was just as beautiful angry as she was at any other time. He had to force himself to concentrate on the subject of their discussion: her relationship with her parents. "You let them walk all over you. Tell them what you think about their attitude. Tell them not to say those things—"

"Don't," Hope said, and lifted her hand as if she could stop his words. "We don't need to talk about this. It always upsets you." She turned, thinking that leaving the room might be the best thing. She didn't want to argue with him, and Eric didn't seem to understand her reasoning at all. But as she moved to leave, she was stopped inadvertently by a surprised Grace, who had heard their exchange of words.

"Excuse me, Grace. I'm going to bed," she said. She longed to hurry past her mother-in-law and escape to the solitude of her bedroom, but Grace's hand closed gently around Hope's forearm.

"Wait, just for a moment. Eric, why are you so hard on her?" Grace asked gently.

"Don't, Mom," Eric warned. "This is something Hope and I have never agreed on, and you don't want to get yourself into the middle of an old argument." He looked at his wife, but she didn't meet his gaze. "I'm sorry if I offended you, Hope. I just hate to see you hurt by them." Then he looked back at his mother. "Her parents don't like me. They never did," he explained. "I guess that makes me overly defensive when they do something hurtful."

Hope stood silently beside Grace, listening to

Eric's comments. Her teeth sank into her lower lip as she considered her parents' discontent with most areas of her life. It had been a long time since she'd thought of how unkind they had been to her husband over the years when he had been nothing but considerate and respectful to them.

Eric continued. "I can accept their feelings toward me, but why Hope allows them to make hurtful comments about the way she lives her life, I really don't understand. I think that if she stood up to them, just once, they'd be so shocked by it, they might back off for a while."

Grace released her gentle hold on Hope and pulled out a nearby kitchen chair to sit down. She looked from her son to her daughter-in-law, each standing on opposite sides of the kitchen, both looking as if they'd prefer being someplace else.

"Eric, I'm sorry my mother and father have been so unfair to you." Hope shook her head regretfully. "There was nothing much I could do about it. From the time we were kids—the more I loved you, the less they liked you."

Eric stared at her, clearly surprised by her admission. "I wasn't looking for an apology."

"But you deserve one," she replied.

"I just want you to stand up for yourself once in a while," he said. "Deference to their position in your life is one thing, but listening to their constant faultfinding is too much. You've been polite and kind to them for as long as I can remember."

Hope was about to respond when Grace intervened on her behalf.

"Do you think it's easy to be kind, polite, even loving to people who are hateful? People who pay little attention to your feelings, your choices in life? How do you think Hope feels when her folks take off on one of their tirades against Christianity, or against you and your marriage?" Grace's questions stung; that was apparent from Eric's downcast expression.

"Mom, I really think she has a right to defend herself."

"And say what? That they're narrow-minded, sharp-tongued people who ought to open their eyes and see her for who she is? A lovely, young Christian mother whose doing a fine job of raising two children, by herself?" Grace emphasized the last two words.

Hope was tired of the struggle she'd known with her parents, but she certainly didn't feel worthy of Grace's compliments. She'd made more mistakes than she would ever want to own up to. Especially to Eric. "Grace, please—"

"Let me finish, dear," Grace interrupted. "Do you think it's weakness that keeps her quiet when she is told how disappointed they are with her?" her mother-in-law asked.

"I don't know," Eric answered. "I hadn't really thought about it."

"Try strength, discipline, sheer willpower. That's

what keeps her from blurting out her feelings. Maybe it would provide a temporary source of comfort to tell them off and be done with them, but what kind of a testimony is that? Would her parents be drawn to the Lord by a Christian daughter who gives them a piece of her mind every time they call?'' Grace's soft voice seemed in such contrast to all she was saying that the impact of her words kept both her son and daughter-in-law silent. "Eric, have you ever sat with Hope while she cried after one of those phone calls?''

Hope's face warmed with an unwanted blush of embarrassment. This was not the kind of thing she wanted said to Eric.

He shook his head. "I remember tears from years ago, but I didn't realize it still had such an impact on her.'' His dark gaze settled on his wife. Hope remained in the doorway, caught between appreciation for her mother-in-law's defense and uneasiness at being praised so profusely and so undeservingly.

"I didn't think so,'' Grace answered, propping an elbow on the table and leaning her head against her hand thoughtfully. "I think, sometimes, strength is not recognized for what it is,'' Grace remarked before standing up. Then she walked over to her son and touched his face with a gentle hand. "A lot of times, whether you men want to admit it or not, the woman is the stronger of the two. Emotionally and spiritually.''

"Words of wisdom from my mother," Eric stated with an easy smile.

Grace's face brightened with a grin of her own. "I'm always willing to stick my nose into other people's business if I think it's necessary, and, so far, with all three of my kids, it's been necessary."

"Right, Mom." Eric folded his arms in front of him and leaned back against the kitchen counter. "And just how do you define 'necessary'?"

"The meaning fluctuates from time to time," she responded, tucking a silvery strand of hair behind her ear. "And from child to child."

"That's what I thought." Then his eyes found Hope's, and confronted her uncertainty. His expression grew serious, wistful. "I'm sorry if I've been too harsh with you, Hope. That was never my intention. I just hate to see you be hurt by anyone."

She nodded. She believed him. His feelings had been something she used to be capable of reading in the depths of his eyes, often even before words were spoken. And tonight, she found that bond existed between them once again.

"Hope, dear," Grace interrupted her daughter-in-law's straying thoughts. "I'm sorry if I was too bold in speaking my thoughts on this matter, but it seemed to me that someone had to point out the facts, and I couldn't trust either one of you to do it."

"It's all right," Hope assured her, swallowing hard. How does one thank someone for defending them above and beyond reason? She wasn't sure she'd ever find an adequate way to do that. "Grace—"

But Grace shook her head. "Don't say anything. I think I know how you feel. Why don't you go on upstairs and check on Beth?"

Eric watched Hope approach his mother and give her a lengthy hug. Then, as Hope turned to leave, he quietly asked, "When are you and Dad leaving for vacation?"

"Anxious to be rid of us?" Grace commented with an eyebrow lifted in question. Hope couldn't resist smiling.

"Yes," he replied with a chuckle. "How soon will you be gone?"

"A cab will be here to pick us up within an hour. We're leaving springtime in Ohio for a few days on a sunny beach in Miami before we go on our cruise."

"I could have taken you to the airport—" Eric began.

"That's not necessary. The cab will do just fine. But maybe you could help us get our luggage loaded. Your dad really shouldn't be lifting anything very heavy."

"Sure, I'll take care of it."

"Good night, Grace. Enjoy your vacation," Hope said, then looked toward her husband. "Good night, Eric." That was something she hadn't said to him in a long time.

"Good night," he responded quietly without looking away from her as she turned and left the room.

"We've already said goodbye to everyone but you, son, so give me a hug," Grace said.

As Eric hugged her warmly, his father walked into the kitchen behind them.

"Time to say 'See you later,' I guess," he said as he extended a hand to Eric for an affectionate squeeze.

"'Bye, Dad."

"Take good care of things while we're gone," his father added. "And don't worry too much about the business. Things will turn in your favor soon enough. They always do."

"Thanks for the thought," Eric replied. "I hope you're right."

"Take care of Hope and the girls," Ed reminded. Then he added in a whisper, "And if you need more time with them, let us know."

"Thanks, Dad. We'll see how it goes," Eric replied with a nod.

Before long a green taxi pulled up in front of the house, and Eric saw that his parents and their belongings—practically *all* of their belongings if the weight of their suitcases was any indication—were safely off to the airport. He slid his hands inside the pockets of his jacket as he walked silently back to the house.

The recent rain had left the spring air smelling clean and damp. The weather had been just like this on the evening he had proposed to Hope. They'd been seniors in college then. They'd walked through a light rain that night to a fast-food restaurant close to campus for a snack. They had laughed and talked about their approaching graduation all the way there.

Somehow, he'd managed to convince Hope to order a kid's meal, just as he'd planned to do. She said she wasn't very hungry and agreed that it would be more than enough to eat—and anyway, she had added with the soft laughter Eric loved, she wanted the cartoon figurine that came with it. But when she disappeared down the hallway toward the ladies' room, Eric opened the sack and substituted a newly purchased diamond ring for the toy that had been included. He smiled at the recollection.

The look on her face when she had discovered the ring, was worth more to him than the ring itself. He'd tried to memorize her reaction—the smile, the tears, the "one-thousand-times *yes!*" They'd been young and crazy about each other, and hadn't even considered the risks of marriage. They trusted God and love and themselves too much to have doubts about their future. They certainly never would have believed back then that things would end up like this—with them in separate bedrooms, separate lives.

Eric walked through the front door into the stillness of the house. He locked the doors before retiring for the night and switched off the lights. As he made his way up the darkened staircase to the second floor, he thought of some of the things Hope had needed him to be over the years. He'd been a good husband, mostly. At least, he thought so. He'd loved her too much for too long to be anything less.

He reached the top step and walked past the guest bedroom, the one Hope now occupied. Then, as he neared the room Beth and Cassie had claimed as their own, he heard the soft words of an old lullaby about rainbows and butterflies.

He stopped to listen. Beth must have had nightmares again. The melody died out just as he neared the doorway to the girls' room. He looked inside to see Beth sleeping peacefully now, with her mother curled up close beside her on the narrow twin bed. Hope had fallen asleep, too, before she'd even finished the last line of the song.

Eric walked into the room and reached for a lightweight blanket from Cassie's empty bed, tossing it over Hope's sleeping form. She didn't actually wake up, but she did touch the blanket and pull it up close to her chin, mumbling a "thank you" in the process.

Eric stood, watching her sleep for a moment or two. She had loved him deeply in the beginning of their marriage. He'd known that; he'd felt it. He couldn't imagine a life without her. Then or now.

When it occurred to him that he'd been standing

there too long, letting his mind run on subjects too close to his heart, he headed for his own bed. He had no way of knowing he would have been happier staying awake. All his dreams that night centered on life with Hope. Good times, bad times. Tender times. A day roller-skating at the rink when they were young. That icy cold kiss that turned warm as they'd knelt together in the snow. Hope weeping in his arms after her parents refused to attend their wedding. He awakened several times in the night—had even reached for her once in his sleepiness, forgetting she no longer shared his bed. Finally, about 3:00 in the morning, he got up and walked to the window to look out into the ink-black sky. The glittering stars looked a million miles away.

"Okay, God," he started his informal attempt at prayer. It had been so long since he'd spoken to the Lord that it felt unnatural, awkward. "If you're trying to get my attention, you've got it. I know I've ruined things with Hope, and I still don't understand why you didn't help Cassie the way I know you could have—" he saw a streak in the sky—a shooting star? "—But I want Hope back again. And I don't really know if you'd be willing, but I could certainly use your help on this. I think you're the only one she really trusts anyway. And, Cassie, I still want her healthy. I want it more than I did the last time I asked you, which was—when? Over a year ago, I guess? But, then, she is almost well this time. I guess I should thank you for that."

Eric stopped talking or praying, or whatever it was he was doing. God hadn't answered his last prayer the way he had expected. It surprised him a little that he was even trying again. He certainly hadn't planned to do so. But he hadn't planned to dream of his wife all night, either, and he had. And this wasn't the first time.

Maybe, a friend had suggested, if Eric had looked for someone else to share his life with... He shook his head and gave a quiet laugh at the irony of the situation. He was a husband accused of unfaithfulness who, in reality, hadn't been unfaithful even once in his life—before *or* after marriage. That wasn't an option as far as Eric was concerned. He loved Hope. And he'd been away from her long enough to realize how *much* he loved her. He had no interest in "looking."

Maybe, if he and Hope had dated others before they married, he could have considered a new relationship more easily. But they had known only each other, and that was a bond Eric wouldn't break. A divorce could be undone just as a marriage could. Legally. They both knew that. But being with another person—that was irreversible. He wouldn't risk that. He didn't want anyone else, and he couldn't, or wouldn't, imagine Hope in another man's arms. He wanted her back where she belonged. In his.

A ringing phone awakened him the next morning before his alarm had buzzed. He reached for the extension close by his bed, but Hope was already talking to whomever the caller was. Eric was about to hang up when he heard the word *hospital*. He stayed on the line as a nurse reported that Cassie had enjoyed a peaceful night, but this morning was asking for her mother already. He heard Hope assure the nurse she'd be there within the hour.

Eric hung up the phone and sat on the edge of the bed. He had two appointments at the office and an apartment building and duplex to show to potential buyers this morning. If Hope needed more help than a ride to school for Beth this morning, she'd have to wait until midafternoon.

He felt thankful that Cassie had experienced a good night there alone at the hospital. It was the kind of news Hope needed to hear. Eric could have thanked the Lord, right then and there. But he didn't. Instead, he took his black dress pants and a shirt with black-and-blue print from the closet along with his favorite dark blue sports coat, placed them on the bed and headed for the shower.

"I'm off to the hospital and then school!" Hope called out, grabbing her purse and car keys. "C'mon, Beth. You're gonna be late again!"

Beth raced down the stairway past her father.

"Hey, slow down on these steps, or you'll fall and we'll be rushing *you* to the hospital," Eric ordered.

"Is this better?" she asked as she slowed her pace a little. She shot him an ornery grin that showed a gap where one baby tooth was missing.

"Much better," Eric answered, and followed her into the kitchen. "Coffee?" he remarked, glancing toward Hope. "I didn't expect you to make this."

"I know—and you're welcome," she replied, admiring his sports coat and tie. He'd always looked good in blue. "C'mon, Beth, your cinnamon toast is on the table. Bring it and grab one of those individual orange juice containers in the fridge. You can have breakfast on the way."

"Teaching, again?" Eric asked, watching Hope adjust the collar on her crimson linen jacket.

"Yes, at Beechmore Elementary."

"So, they have a new principal there now," Eric remarked, reaching into the dish rack for a clean cup. He looked up at her.

"Yes, remember? I mentioned Greg Shelton to you the other day when we had that discussion in the hospital cafeteria. He replaced Marjorie White, who went on maternity leave this year." Hope pulled the tab to open the juice carton Beth had handed her. "Why?"

Eric poured hot coffee into his cup. "No reason," he answered.

But Hope had her doubts. Maybe one of the girls had mentioned something about their principal. Hope wasn't certain, but she knew she didn't have time to think about it now. "Let's go," she urged, and handed the open carton to Beth.

Oh, there was one more thing she had meant to mention to Eric: during that phone call from her parents last night, they had informed her that her brother, Harry, was coming to Columbus for a visit. Beth opened the door, and the cool morning air blew into the kitchen. No, Hope decided, she wouldn't mention it now. He wouldn't be happy with this news. No sense in ruining his entire day.

Hope and Beth arrived at school on time after a brief stop to see Cassie, then went their separate ways for the day—Beth to first grade and Hope to second. The morning flew by, and soon Hope joined some other teachers for lunch in the cafeteria. The conversation flowed smoothly, and the break from the kids was pleasant as lunchroom monitors supervised mealtime for the children. Suddenly the course of the casual discussion changed drastically with a surprising remark from the principal, who was seated across from Hope.

"Why don't you sever your ties with Eric Granston and move on?"

She glanced over at Greg Shelton. He was tall with dark blond hair and eyes that were a friendly blue. Discussing her marriage with him was not something Hope wanted. She opened her mouth to respond, but the friend seated next to her beat her to the draw.

"Sever her ties?" Marcia remarked. "C'mon,

Greg. What do you know about a single mother trying to survive financially on her own out here in the real world? Talk about stress! Ask me. I've been doing it for three years. If she can hang on to Eric enough to get the help she needs—financial or whatever—and yet still have some freedom...she'd be crazy to let go of that.''

Hope was about to explain that she was not hanging on to Eric for money, that the meaning of marriage went way beyond that, when Greg responded.

"All I'm saying is that if Hope wants out of that relationship, she should get out. End it once and for all so she's free to carve out another life for herself." He returned his gaze to Hope, who had yet to respond to anything. "I want her to know there are other options available, if she's interested."

Marcia's talk was silenced as she and the five other teachers seated at their table looked from the principal to the substitute teacher whose light blue eyes had widened in astonishment.

"Greg—" Hope started, then stopped. What was he saying? And why was he saying it in front of a table full of their co-workers? "We're friends, that's all," she finally stated, wanting that fact to be clear to him and everyone else within hearing range. "Why would you say—"

"Why would I say this, here? Now? In front of so many people? Because I want this to be an out-in-the-open matter with us—no gossip or whispering behind our backs. You and I have worked together enough to become friends over the past year, but it could be more than that, if you'd let it. And I know you well enough to realize that you won't let it develop into anything more until you are free of Eric Granston."

Hope, stunned, sat silently for a moment, her fair complexion allowing her cheeks to burn with color. "Greg..." she started, "I'll never be 'free' of Eric. I'm his wife. I have children with him—"

"But he's not the only man you could have a future with." Greg's words were gentle, but she was too startled by his announcement to reply. Over the months she had known him, he'd been a good listener when they'd talked, a kind and considerate friend who'd even visited Cassie in the hospital several times. He was a tenderhearted father, raising his two young children alone, a widower sought after by several of the single moms Hope knew— including her friend Marcia. And, although the thought that his interest in her might go beyond the walls of this school had crossed her mind, and Grace's, Hope hadn't expected to have it spelled out for her so plainly, so clearly. Or so publicly.

"Greg, you're a Christian, aren't you?" Marcia asked sharply.

Greg's reply was very matter-of-fact. "That's why I'm trying to do this the most appropriate way I know how."

Hope placed her fork on her tray. The creamed chicken on biscuits had suddenly lost its appeal as she listened to the exchange. Words involving her future. *Hers!*

"We can't talk about this here—now. Greg, if you wanted to say such a thing to me, it should have been done privately. Not here in the lunch-room."

"With someone else, that might be true, but not with you, Hope. You need things to be out in the open. I can't even have a private moment with you the way things are now. You wouldn't allow it, not while you're still married." Greg paused, glancing at the curious faces all turned in his direction, apparently waiting for another interesting tidbit. "So, to prevent rumors from flying, which they are known to do around here, I'm saying this publicly, letting everyone who's listening know there's nothing going on between us. Not now. But I'm interested in you, if you are ever free to consider a future with someone else."

"Are you implying marriage?" Marcia asked bluntly.

"*Marcia!* How could you ask—" Hope started to reply, but Greg cut her off.

"Yes," he stated as simply as if he were giving the time of day. "Marriage."

Hope swallowed back the words that wanted to rush out. What was he talking about? Had he lost his mind? The man hadn't even been alone with her more than a moment here and there. How could he possibly know he wanted to marry her? "But, Greg—"

"I don't want an answer from you now. Just think it over—we'll talk later." Then Greg gave a long sigh. "So, now that's taken care of, maybe we can all finish our lunches and let things get back to normal."

"Back to normal?" Marcia remarked between bites of peas. "What fun is that?"

But Hope had lost her appetite completely. Greg Shelton had made an offer of marriage that she hadn't even seen coming. She recalled that they had discussed plans for the future on occasion during the lunch break, but so had everyone else present at the table. And Grace had suggested that Greg had something like this in mind when Hope mentioned the conversations to her, but Hope had dismissed her mother-in-law's notion as silly. It looked like Grace had been right; Hope was the one who had misjudged the situation.

She excused herself from the table and retreated with a cup of coffee to the classroom for a few minutes of solitude. Greg was a friend—that was all, wasn't it? She ran over bits and pieces of conversations she'd had with him over recent months. They'd been friends. She couldn't think of anything she'd done that would have led him to think otherwise. Propping her elbows on the huge wooden desk she sat behind, she buried her face in her hands. What a dilemma this could be. Beth would hear about this as the news traveled through the school. Eric might even hear of it and accuse her of an inappropriate relationship with Greg. Not that he'd personally care, but parents sometimes lost custody of their kids over issues like this. She couldn't bear the thought of not raising her girls. But then she thought of Eric and the kind of man he was, and she knew he wouldn't take the children away from her—no matter what happened between the two of them.

A bell rang, signaling the end of lunch and the return of her class to the room. Maybe she should tell Eric about this. Soon. Before he heard it from someone else. She stood up and picked up a piece of white chalk to write a dozen new spelling words on the dusty green board behind her chair. What would Eric's reaction be? And how would she handle it, whatever it was?

"We're back, Mrs. Granston!" one of the children called out as several of them burst into the room, still vibrant with energy although half of their day was behind them.

Hope smiled, blinking back the sting of unbidden tears that appeared at the mention of the name. Eric's name. Would it always belong to her?

The day had seemed long from that point on. By the time the dismissal bell rang, Beth had already heard the news, and Hope was bombarded with questions.

"Mom, when are you going to marry Mr. Shelton? Why didn't you tell Cassie and me about it? Why do you want to raise his kids for him?"

Hope had been quick to explain that it wasn't true, that she had *not* agreed to a marriage. But Beth spilled the story to Cassie as soon as they walked into her hospital room, and Hope spent the next several minutes separating facts from rumors. Despite Hope's clarification attempt, however, Cassie was visibly upset.

"What about Dad? Have you said anything about this to him? He's not gonna like this one bit."

Hope reached into her purse for the two aspirins she usually carried with her for days like this, and she paused to wonder how many days like this there could be in a lifetime. She excused herself to the water fountain long enough to take the pills and get a momentary break from her kids. Why, oh, why had Greg Shelton thought he needed to announce his feelings publicly? A nice card in the mail with an RSVP would have been easier, Hope thought with a smile. Ridiculous, but easier.

"Mom, Dad was here earlier and he didn't say anything about this. Are you sure he knows about—"

The questions began again as soon as she entered the room. "Girls, listen to me," Hope began as she sank into the nearby green vinyl chair. "Dad knows nothing about this. Your father and I are still married, and I have no plans to marry anyone else. Ever.''

That turned out to be the wrong thing to say: as the girls started in with questions about what their mother wanted in life. To be married? Not to be married? To be with Dad? Not to be with Dad? Hope was at the end of her patience when her sister-in-law, Angela, poked her head into the room and asked if she was interrupting anything.

''Yes!'' Hope exclaimed with a sigh. ''And thank you!''

Angela frowned. ''Rough day?''

''You could say that.''

The girls greeted Angela and shared the biggest news item of the day from Beechmore Elementary.

''Wow,'' Angela remarked, sitting down on the edge of the bed. ''And I was just stopping in to see how Cassie's feeling and to tell you about Adam adopting the children. I had no idea so much was going on.''

''Adopting? Angela, that's wonderful,'' Hope enthused. ''I knew you'd been thinking about it for a long time, but it's great that you're moving ahead with it.''

''Well, I'm jumping the gun here a little bit. We haven't actually filed any papers yet. But I did send a letter to the children's grandparents, the Sanders, to see if we could have—if not their blessing, at least their approval on this matter. Until I hear from them, we're not going to proceed.''

"Do you think they'll agree to let the children have Adam's last name?"

Angela shrugged and with a halfhearted grin said, "I don't know. We'll just wait and see. I'll let you know what happens. But for now, tell me more about Greg Shelton and this proposal of sorts."

"Can you believe it?" Hope asked. "He said all of that, about marriage and everything, right in front of everyone at the table."

Angela opened her arms to give Cassie a hug. "Yes, Hope, with Greg Shelton, I can believe that. He's not the kind of guy I would expect to do things in any way other than right out in the open." She paused. "What about Eric? Have you told him yet?"

"Dad doesn't know," Beth chimed in. "I bet he'll be surprised."

Angela and Hope exchanged a look of uncertainty. Neither one knew what reaction to expect.

"It's probably a good thing this happened," Angela said with a slight shrug. "He needs to know he's losing you—*really* losing you. Nothing can say it any clearer to him than an offer of marriage from another man."

"But that's *not* the way Mom and Dad got engaged, is it, Mom?" Cassie asked quickly. "You were in love. You were really *excited* when he gave you that ring. Don't you remember? You've told us that story a couple of times."

Hope nodded. She remembered, too well. She glanced down at her fingers, and the gold band and diamond that she'd worn for so many years. That miserable night when Eric had walked out of their house, Hope had taken them off purely out of anger, and placed them in the bottom of her jewelry box. But she couldn't bring herself to leave them there, so back onto her finger they had gone that very same evening. She was glad of her decision because the next time she saw Eric, he was wearing his, too. And he wore it still, even after six months apart.

What Hope longed for was the commitment and love those endless circles represented. Eric's reaction to the news about Greg Shelton's proposal could tell her all she needed to know about his feelings for her. Then, she needed to find a way to tell Eric the facts about that day at the pool that she'd kept from him for so long. They wouldn't have a chance unless she did so.

"There are many better ways to become engaged than being asked in front of half a dozen people during lunch in a cafeteria," Angela remarked, studying Hope's troubled expression. Then she turned her attention to Beth. "Maybe you girls should let your mom be the one to tell your father about this. What do you think, Hope?"

"Yes," Hope was quick to acknowledge. "Please, don't say anything about this until I've explained it to him."

"When Dad was in earlier, he said it had been a

really good day at the office,'' Cassie said. "He said he was looking forward to spending some time with Beth tonight when he finally got home. He's working kinda late.''

"Eric doesn't even know yet that my brother is coming for a visit tomorrow. So…Greg Shelton *and* Harry Ryan. I guess I have two things I dread telling Eric tonight,'' Hope commented.

"Only two?'' Angela asked, raising her dark eyebrows in question. Her blue eyes reminded Hope of the color of the pool water that long-ago day—a day Angela remembered, too.

"Yes,'' Hope responded, flashing a frown at her sister-in-law for bringing up an old subject. "That's all.''

The girls seemed to have missed the negative exchange between the women. Beth's grin widened as she announced, "I like Uncle Harry. He's funny.''

Angela smiled back. "I don't think that's the adjective your father would use to describe Uncle Harry.''

"I'm quite sure that it's not,'' Hope added. She sighed theatrically as she thought of the unpleasant possibilities. "I can hardly wait to get home.''

"Good afternoon,'' Eric said as his brother Rob walked through the front door of the real estate office. "I wasn't expecting to see you today.''

"I know. I had to come to Columbus for a meeting so I thought I'd stop in," Rob replied.

"So, what's up?" Eric relaxed in the swivel chair he was seated in behind his wide oak desk. "Are you here to buy that big apartment complex I've been trying to move for a couple of months?"

"Nope, sorry. Nothing like that."

When Rob hesitated after those words, Eric sensed that there apparently was a specific reason for his brother's arrival here today. "Are you okay?" Eric asked.

"Yeah," Rob replied. "It's just this new position I've been offered...the moving away..." Rob walked to the window near the large desk and looked out.

"Mom told me about it," Eric said. "She said it's a big offer—large church, more money, more prestige. You're not happy about that?"

"I don't know how I feel about it. That's the problem, I guess." Rob turned his head to look at his brother. "Have you ever been unsure of something? I mean really, totally, unsure?"

Eric thought for a moment, wanting to give as honest an answer as he could. "There've been lots of times like that," he said. "In the business, with the kids...even with Hope. Sometimes you just make the best judgment call you can and go from there."

"But on the really big issues—like leaving

Hope—were you sure that was the only thing left to do?''

Eric frowned. "No. Not at all. Leaving Hope was the biggest mistake I've ever made in my life." But he couldn't imagine Rob considering something like that. "You and Micah aren't having problems, are you?"

"No, nothing like that. Micah's wonderful," Rob replied. He sunk his hands into his pockets.

"Has she hinted that she's against this move?" Eric asked.

"No…she'd go wherever I wanted—"

A feminine voice interrupted their conversation with a greeting. "Hi, guys!"

Eric and Rob both turned to see their sister, Angela, entering the office with her three-year-old daughter in tow. She added, "Congratulations on the new job. Mom told us all about it. Arizona, huh?"

Rob smiled. "I think Mom's been telling everyone. It's good to see you two." He leaned over to pick up little Andrea, a pint-size combination package of Angela and her husband Adam. Andrea had gorgeous blue eyes like her mother and her father's golden hair.

"She looks like an angel sent straight from heaven," Eric commented as he studied his niece, now nestled snugly in Uncle Rob's arms.

Angela laughed. "You wouldn't have said that

last night if you'd seen the temper tantrum the 'little angel' was having.''

Eric laughed, too. "What was she mad about?"

"She found a candy bar in Heather's book bag, and she wanted it for a bedtime snack." Angela crossed her arms and feigned an angry glare at her youngest child. "Not my idea of a healthy choice."

Andrea giggled at her mother's funny expression. "Mommy, you're silly!" she insisted. Angela reached out and took the child from her uncle's arms.

"So tell me about the job," Angela said. "You're not really moving away from us, are you? All the way across the country, like Mom said?"

Rob shrugged his shoulders slightly. "Looks like we are. It's a great offer—a much larger church with a big, beautiful parsonage."

"Well, be warned. No one in this family wants to see you go," Angela said before turning to Eric. "I just saw Cassie. She seemed to be feeling well."

"She's doin' great and should be home soon," Eric answered with a genuine smile. "No fever yesterday."

"She'll be glad to get out of that hospital," Rob remarked.

Eric nodded. "And I'll be glad to be staying in the same house with her again for a while." Eric didn't miss the look exchanged by his siblings. "It's a temporary setup for now, you guys."

Angela smiled; Rob didn't.

"Mom told us you were staying there," Angela commented, still smiling. "How are things between you and Hope?"

"They're the same as they were before I moved some of my clothes in there. Living under the same roof hasn't changed anything yet." He wished it had. He looked from Angela's inquisitive eyes to Rob's. Angela was asking more than the simple question implied. And Rob was asking nothing.

Angela persisted. "Eric, don't you think if you tried—"

"I am trying," he interrupted. "And I'm hoping it will make a difference. But I don't know."

Just then, Andrea wriggled out of her mother's arms and ran toward the door. "Andi, don't open that door! You wait for Mommy." Angela returned her attention to Eric. "Sorry. I'll try not to ask things like that. I remember how it felt to have a marriage fall apart." She reached out, touching her brother's arm gently. "Forgive me."

Eric nodded without speaking as Angela said her goodbyes, then took Andrea's hand and walked out the front door.

"Where's your receptionist?" Rob asked as Angela left the office. The front desk sat conspicuously empty with the computer screen on and a half-empty cup of coffee beside it.

"She went to the post office to mail some packages. I hope she comes back before you leave. I'd like you to meet her," Eric said. He glanced out the window to see if the woman was returning, but there was no sign of her. "She'll remind you of Mom." Eric looked over at his brother for a reaction, knowing Rob would probably be careful not to give one. And he was right.

"Hired a new one?" his brother responded casually.

"It seemed like a good idea," Eric said. He remembered the angry words exchanged between him and Hope the night he had left. And the accusations that he hadn't deserved.

Rob nodded his head without replying.

"Listen, I know you've heard the story...Hope's side of everything. But there was nothing going on between the receptionist and me. Nothing except a stupid flirtation," Eric explained defensively.

Rob shrugged. "Maybe that didn't seem like much to you, but to your wife—"

"I know. It was stupid. And wrong. But at the time I was surprised she even noticed," Eric interrupted, and then frowned. That thought hadn't occurred to him before now. Was that what he had tried to do? Make her notice?

"Maybe that's what you were aiming for? Hope's attention?" Rob suggested.

"I don't know. Maybe. But that sounds like such juvenile behavior," Eric remarked.

"Don't be so hard on yourself, Eric," Rob commented. "Just discuss it with Hope. It might make a difference."

"I will talk to her about it, when I get the chance. That's not the kind of subject I can bring up easily, you know. And she probably still won't believe me."

"Give her a chance, Eric. Maybe she'll *want* to believe you this time."

"I wish she would," Eric replied. "I miss her, Rob. I know this will sound strange, but I think I actually miss her more now that I'm with her—in Mom and Dad's house—than I did when I rarely saw her. Trading the girls back and forth on the weekends, and passing each other in the doorway at the hospital didn't hurt as much as being around her now—daily, nightly." Eric sighed audibly and leaned back in his chair. "There's this hedge she keeps around herself...something that makes her more withdrawn from me than I'd ever have believed she could be. It started right after Cassie hurt her back."

"Have you asked her about it?"

Eric nodded. "I've tried, but she won't open up. She feels guilty about Cassie's injury, about taking her to the pool that afternoon, and I've told her every way I know how that it's not her fault." He shrugged. "And Cassie doesn't remember anything about that day, which doesn't help."

"Do you want me to talk to her for you?" Rob offered.

"No," Eric said. "Thanks, but I've got to do this myself. I want her back, Rob—back the way things used to be. And I've got the next two weeks to do it."

"There's something else in your life that needs to get back to the way it used to be, Eric," Rob stated matter-of-factly.

Eric nodded with an acknowledging smile. "I know. When I left the church and let my relationship with God fall apart, that didn't do anything to help my marriage."

"It's up to you to repair that, you know," Rob reminded him.

"I know, and believe me it's on my mind a lot. I'm just not quite there yet."

Rob nodded in understanding. "I have to be going. Micah's waiting for me."

"What about Arizona? Do you think you'll go?"

"I don't know," Rob answered, "but we'll have to decide soon. I didn't even ask about you. How's the business doing without Dad around?"

"It's been slow." Eric slid some papers into a black briefcase, then switched on the answering machine beside the phone on his desk. "Hope and I sold our house when we separated. We split the equity, and I banked my half. I figured the day would come when I'd want to do more than fritter it away on daily expenses." He turned off the overhead lights, but the sunlight shining through the windows still filled the room as he motioned for Rob. The two of them walked toward the back door.

"I can always fall back on those savings when times get tough."

"'When times get tough,'" Rob repeated. "When we were kids and 'times got tough,' that usually meant eating a lot of chili without much meat in it, and homemade cookies instead of the ones from the supermarket."

Eric grinned. "I always liked Mom's better anyway."

"Me, too," Rob agreed. There was silence for a moment between them before Rob made a quiet offer. "I could lend you some cash if you need it."

"I'm sure you could," Eric responded with a genuine chuckle. "You probably have money tucked away in places that even God and Micah don't know about."

Rob smiled, but his words were serious. "No one hides anything from God, Eric. And as for Micah, I don't keep secrets from my wife."

Eric considered his brother's words as he drove away from his office late that afternoon toward Cassie and the hospital. He had messed things up with Hope, and he knew it. But it hadn't had anything to do with secrets. Unless Hope had something *she* was withholding. And, that, he suddenly realized, was a possibility. The withdrawing from him rather than drawing closer to him during difficult days had been very unlike her, and there had to be some explanation for it.

He drove into the hospital parking lot and, taking a time-stamped ticket from the machine, he headed for a parking space. Within minutes, he was tapping at the closed door to his daughter's hospital room.

"Come in." It was Hope's voice.

Eric stepped inside. "Hi, princess," he said, and leaned forward to kiss Cassie's smiling face.

"Hi, Dad. How are you?" Cassie looked beautiful. Her cheeks had more color, her smile was wide, and her speech had that familiar singsonginess to it that Eric adored.

"I'm fine, babe. The question is, how are *you?*"

"Great! I beat Mom at Make a Million again," she replied, referring to her favorite board game. "For about the tenth time in a row this week."

Hope came out of the tiny bathroom in the corner of Cassie's room, smiling and drying her hands on a paper towel that she promptly discarded in the trash can near the door. "You beat me because you buy every property you land on, with no regard for whether or not you can afford it, and, for some strange reason, that works for you." She patted Cassie's arm and returned to her seat beside the bed. "You're destined to buy and sell real estate just like your grandfather and your father." Hope looked up at Eric, the first time she had done so since he'd entered the room.

"Let's pray she's a little better at it than I've been lately," he remarked with a grin.

"Pray?" Hope repeated instantly, raising a hand

to touch the gold cross at her throat. Eric regretted his slip of the tongue. This was not a good subject to embark on. "I didn't know you recommended that to anyone these days." She studied him rather cautiously, Eric decided. But he smiled in response to her remark.

"Occasionally, I fall back into old habits," he replied before looking away. "Where's Beth?"

"At a friend's house. I'll pick her up on my way home," Hope replied.

Eric nodded, then turned his attention to Cassie. "And you will be successful, young lady, selling property or whatever you do, because of that beautiful smile."

"Dad, you have a charming smile yourself, you know," Cassie said suddenly.

Eric laughed heartily. "Charming, huh?" He sat down in the chair near the window. "Now, that's something I've not heard before."

"Well, it's true. That's one of the things that Mom liked about you when you were young. Isn't it, Mom?"

Eric watched Hope's expression change from one of surprise to obvious embarrassment, but she nodded her head reluctantly. "Cassie was asking about how we met…so I told her…about us."

Eric was still smiling when he turned back to his daughter. "You're quite the snoop these days, aren't you?" he teased, remembering his own recent conversation with Cassie on the same topic.

"I'm just curious," Cassie quickly defended herself. "About my heritage—you know, my roots. We were studying that in school just before I got sick this time."

Eric nodded as though he accepted her explanation, but he lifted an eyebrow sharply to let Cassie know he wasn't quite that gullible.

"Well, Cassie," Hope interrupted, "I need to get going. Your sister is waiting on me."

Eric found it refreshing to see her in good spirits, with almost a shimmer in her blue eyes. "I'll be home later to help with Beth," he offered.

Hope nodded. "'Bye, sweetie," Hope whispered to Cassie, and gave her a quick kiss. "Are you sure you want to stay all night by yourself again?"

"I'm sure, Mom. I'll be okay." Cassie's smile was a sly one as she leaned back against two fluffy pillows and watched her mother disappear through the doorway.

"What do you look so smug about, dear daughter?" Eric asked, propping his feet up on a small stand he had been using for a footstool. "Are you that happy about spending a night alone again?"

"That…and you and Mom." Her face nearly beamed with confidence.

"Well, it's not exactly me and Mom, yet," Eric admitted quietly, not wanting to allow Cassie's daydreaming to kick into high gear just yet. "Give us some time."

Time. Alone together. That was what he wanted and rarely had with Hope.

But for whatever reason, Cassie was undeterred. "Happily ever after," she commented. "That's how your love story will end."

"I hope so, princess," Eric replied.

"Now, checkers or Scrabble?" She reached for the games stacked on the stand behind her bed.

"Scrabble? That's a different one. Who gave you that game?" he asked as he pulled his chair up closer.

"Grandma. She wanted to give me a gift before she left on the cruise—in case she drowned or was kidnapped by pirates in the Caribbean." Cassie giggled. "She wanted me to have something to help remember her."

Cassie took the lid off the box she'd placed on the bed, and engaged her father in a lengthy game. They were interrupted about an hour later by visitors. "Hi, Cassie," said a soft voice, and Cassie looked up at the sound.

"Aunt Micah! I'm so glad to see you!"

Micah enveloped Cassie in a huge hug. "I'm happy to see you, too, sweetheart. How are you feeling?"

"Pretty good," she answered, "and I've got lots of energy."

"That's wonderful! We wanted to stop by to see

you, but we won't stay long," she began. "How are you, Eric?"

"Fine, thanks. Where's the rest of that family of yours?"

"Rob will be here in a minute. He stopped at the gift shop to pick up something. And Dad's down in the lobby with the kids." Micah reached into the oversize bag she carried over one shoulder. "Look, Cass. I brought pictures of you and Beth at the twins' birthday party. Remember? I'd forgotten about the roll of film until I found it in the camera last week. I just had it developed."

Soon Cassie was thumbing through the snapshots, laughing at some, frowning at others. Micah asked, "Where's Hope?"

"Probably at home with Beth by now," Eric answered.

"Rob told me you were staying at the house," Micah remarked. "That's good because I think Hope can use some help while your parents are gone."

"I know," he responded. "That's what I'm trying to do." He smiled at his little girl. "I think I'll go downstairs to see if I can find your Uncle Rob." He was glad to get out from under Micah's scrutiny. She'd made no secret of her opinions about his separation from Hope. And he'd made no real attempt to explain any of it to Micah—or anyone else, for that matter. He'd left because Hope had asked him to go. It wasn't what he had wanted.

"Eric, over here!" Rob called as he saw his brother walk into the gift shop. Rob was standing close to the cash register, paying for his purchase.

"Hi," Eric greeted him. "Ready to see Cassie?"

"Yep. I picked up a couple of things for her. Why don't you go home and get some rest? Micah and I can stay here until Hope comes back. She's spending the nights with Cassie, isn't she?"

"Most of them," Eric responded. "But tonight Cassie wants to try it alone again, so Hope's staying home."

"She'll be fine, Eric, and I'm sure the hospital would call if she needed you or Hope for any reason."

Eric nodded. He knew his brother was right. "I am tired," he commented. "Maybe I'll say goodnight to Cassie, and go home to spend a little time with Beth before she goes to bed."

"Good idea," Rob commented as they walked out of the gift shop and headed toward Cassie's room.

And maybe, Eric added silently, he would find the right time, the right place...and the right things to say to his wife. Tonight.

"Eight o'clock, Hope? Her bedtime didn't used to be so early," Eric said as he pulled his tie free of his shirt and unfastened the top two buttons. Then he glanced over at the clock on top of the television. It had been a productive day at the office, and Eric had arrived home only minutes earlier. Beth had come running to see her father as he opened the front door. "She's not even tired yet."

"Yeah, Mom. I'm not even tired," Beth joined in.

"Eric, I appreciate your help but you can't disrupt her schedule whenever it suits you. It's hard on her." But, mostly, Hope knew, the person it was hard on was herself. She had planned to get Beth to bed on time tonight. They both could use a good night's sleep. And there was that matter of Greg Shelton's marriage proposal she needed to discuss with Eric—privately. She crossed her arms in front of her and wondered if Eric's mouth would curve into that infuriating half smile he sometimes had when he knew she was miffed about something. "She has to go to bed earlier now because she has to get up earlier than she used to. She usually bathes in the morning—"

"Can't she do that at bedtime like she used to do? Why did you change things?" Eric asked without smiling.

Hope cleared her throat, fighting back the impulse to argue, at least until Beth left the room. "I changed things because I have to do what works best for me. Helping the girls with their baths in the morning is easier than doing it at night when we're all tired and grumpy." Eric had helped the girls with their baths when he'd been a part of their everyday lives. Could he have forgotten that so easily?

Eric slid a hand into his pocket as he winked at Beth. "If Mom says it's bedtime, then it's bedtime."

"But, Daaaddy," Beth protested.

He swatted her lightly on the bottom and nodded toward the staircase. "Go on, before we both get into trouble with your mother. We'll be up in a minute to tuck you in."

Beth began climbing the stairs slowly, dragging her favorite stuffed bear behind her, bumping its little head against each step on the way. Eric and Hope watched her go.

Then Eric smiled. "That bear is gonna need some aspirin—"

"You're gonna need some aspirin if you keep questioning my rules around here. Do you have any idea how hard it is to raise two children alone and keep things running smoothly?" Hope's unexpected outburst surprised her almost as much as it did Eric. She hadn't meant to be so emotional, but Eric could be so calm, so casual at times like this, and she wanted something else from him. Concern, consideration…something she couldn't quite define.

Eric opened his mouth to respond, but Hope continued to let her feelings be known. "And don't tell me that having them on Saturday and Sunday is anything like having them all the time. There's no comparing the daily parenting I do with them to whatever it is you do with them on your weekends. You know, visitation isn't supposed to be like a holiday every single time you have them.''

Eric frowned. "It's not. It's—"

"It's like Christmas or a birthday or all-As-on-their-grade-card day every time they're with you. They come home with new toys or books, and they've eaten pizza three meals in a row. How do you think life with me stacks up against family fun with Dad?''

"Hope, I'm not trying to do that. I just—"

"You just what? Want to be more fun than I am? Well, guess what? You win.'' Hot, angry tears stung her eyes, but she blinked hard. "You don't have a clue what my life has been like these past six months, do you? And you probably don't even care,'' she remarked, turning on her heels to follow her daughter's path to the second floor. Greg Shelton wants me; why can't you? she thought miserably as she left the room.

"I care, Hope,'' Eric answered as she stormed up the stairs. "Honestly.'' But she was hurrying to join Beth, and she didn't respond to his reply. He wasn't totally sure she'd been aware of it.

Where had he gone wrong? He thought she was doing a wonderful job with the kids. He found no fault in the way she was bringing them up.

Eric ascended the stairs a short time later, after checking the doors and turning out the lights. He moved quietly through the darkened second floor toward his bedroom. But as he passed Beth's room, he heard her call to him.

"Daddy, why can't you sit with me for a while?"

He paused in the doorway. "Beth, your mother likes to have that time with you—"

"No, you go ahead," Hope said softly. She wished now that she could take back the bitter words she'd spoken. If only she didn't love him so much, her emotions wouldn't climb and dip the way they did. But she couldn't explain away her behavior. "Beth wants you to be with her, and it will give me a chance to call the hospital and check on Cassie. I don't like leaving her alone again tonight."

"But she wants to be able to stay at night on her own, Hope. She's doing fine."

"Well, I'm going to call just to be sure. Good night, Beth." She leaned over and kissed the child on the forehead.

"Will you be going to the hospital, Mom?"

Hope shook her head and smiled. "Not unless Cassie needs me. And Dad is right. She's probably doing just fine without me. Her favorite nurse is on duty tonight."

"Trudy?" Eric asked.

Hope's expression was one of surprise. She nodded.

"Didn't think I'd know that, huh?" he asked without humor. What did Hope think of him, anyway? That he didn't worry about his daughter sleeping alone in that skyscraper hospital with cold tile floors and doors that swung open unexpectedly? He'd spent plenty of nights there with Cassie in the past. He knew how still it would sound, how lonely it could feel in the early hours of the morning, even if there was someone whose first name you knew in the bed next to yours.

"No, I didn't," Hope admitted. "I guess I didn't think a man would pay attention to small details like that."

"You mean, you didn't think *I* would pay attention, don't you?" Eric asked in a quiet voice.

Hope nodded. The error was hers. "I guess so."

"Sometimes I'll surprise you like that," he responded, his mouth curving into a smile that appealed to Hope much more than she wanted to admit. Then Eric continued. "My sister has more confidence in me than you do. She views me as one of the 'new sensitive' males."

"But Angela hasn't lived with you since you were—what? Eighteen, maybe? I wonder what she based her findings on?"

"Certainly not our separation," Eric replied, studying Hope's startled blue gaze. "I don't think Angela's ever going to forgive me for that."

Hope's mouth turned down in sad response, and an acute sense of loss rifled through Eric, stronger than ever before. He looked away from her for a moment to regain his composure. There was so much he needed to say. But not here, not now in front of their daughter. He looked toward Beth. "Ready to sleep?" he asked needlessly.

"No!" came his daughter's emphatic answer, as if there had been any chance she'd agree.

"Well, I am. So, get comfortable, and I'll sit here with you until you go to sleep." He looked toward Hope again, but saw only soft blond hair and the back of her rainbow-striped robe as she gave a quiet good-night before disappearing through the doorway.

Joseph's coat of many colors, Eric had nicknamed that robe. He and the girls had given it to Hope on Christmas two years ago. Hope loved it; he had known she would. And she looked as beautiful in it tonight as she had that Christmas morning. He stood staring at the empty doorway until Beth's statement cut through his thoughts.

"Turn out the lights, Dad, or I can't sleep."

And he did so. But lights or no lights, he knew *he* wouldn't get much sleep. Not with so much left unsaid.

Chapter Four

⁓

Being able to slip out of the house early the next morning without encountering Eric in the kitchen was a break Hope welcomed. She was still upset about last night. She'd said all the wrong things, mostly in frustration because she hadn't found the courage to tell him about Greg Shelton. How could she tell him when she was so afraid of his response? What if he was glad? Relieved? Grateful? What reaction would she see in his eyes?

Hope continued the walk down the hallway of the hospital, opening the door to Cassie's hospital room so she and Beth could step inside.

"Mom? You should be on your way to school," Cassie said, looking up at the clock beside her bed.

"Yes, we need to go, but I wanted to see how you were doing this morning."

"I'm fine. The doctor has already been in to see me."

"Good. Then I'll call him later. Are you sure you're okay? Did you sleep well last night?"

"Yes, Mom, I'm fine. Now, go before you make Beth late for school!"

"Okay, okay." Hope kissed her older girl and took Beth's hand in hers. Then it was off to get Beth to class on time and back home for Hope to do some housework before she picked up Harry at the airport. He could have driven in from out of state in less than ten hours, but that wasn't Harry's style. Why drive when you could fly?

Hope shook her head as she thought of her sibling. He was divorced and, according to Hope's parents, he paid little attention to his sons, of whom his former wife had custody. He rarely had any significant money of his own, and when he did, he didn't have it long.

She still hadn't told Eric that her brother would be here. Today. She'd have to tell him about Harry, even if she couldn't make herself tell him about Greg Shelton. The girls would probably take care of that soon enough on their own.

Less than an hour later, Eric came downstairs as Hope was running the vacuum over the living room carpet. She turned the sweeper off and pushed it to the side. "Good morning," she said, concentrating on the cord she was rewinding. She had to tell him. Now.

"'Morning," Eric replied. "I had about a dozen calls to make. Since you and Beth were already gone, I decided to take care of most of them from here. I'm going to stop at the office, and then I have a meeting downtown in about an hour."

"Okay," she responded, then took a deep breath. "Eric, wait…. Harry is coming for a visit," she said, looking up to see his reaction although she already knew what to expect.

"If you're trying to brighten my day, that didn't do it," Eric said tersely. "I hope you didn't tell him he could stay here."

"No, no…nothing like that. He'll be getting a hotel room for the few days he'll be in town. The thought of asking him to stay here didn't even cross my mind," she answered truthfully. Eric and Harry didn't get along well enough to be this close to each other for more than a few minutes at a time. "He'll be here later today."

Eric closed the file he'd been looking through, and reached for his keys. "Let me know his schedule once he arrives, and I'll try to stay out of his way. You'll have a much better visit if I do." He glanced at her, meeting her gaze where she stood by the staircase. "Do you know why he's coming?" he asked. Harry had an ulterior motive for every move he made in life; Eric was convinced of it.

"Just to visit," Hope replied. "We haven't seen him for a couple of years."

"That's what I mean. You haven't heard from him in all this time, and now, suddenly, he's coming here. Doesn't that seem odd to you?"

She shook her head. "Not really. Maybe he just misses us." She pushed the sweeper into the hallway closet.

"Maybe," Eric said. But he doubted it. Whenever Harry had shown up in the past, which had been rarely, trouble had followed. But, Eric considered, he couldn't be coming to stir up marital problems, could he? None any worse than what they were already experiencing, at any rate. Then he had another thought. "Maybe he's coming to celebrate the possibility of getting rid of me as a brother-in-law. I'm sure the thought would please him."

So, now it was only a possibility? Hope smoothed her brow with both hands, fighting off the beginning of a headache. "Let's just assume he's coming to see his sister and let it go at that," she replied in a soft voice. "Okay?"

"Okay," he said more calmly. But it wasn't okay. Harry probably loved Hope and the girls, but that wasn't the only reason he would show up now. Eric wasn't going to give his brother-in-law the benefit of the doubt this time. Harry had disappointed Hope several times before; Eric hated to think of her being hurt again. There was only so much he could do to prevent it. "Hope, please, be careful where Harry's concerned," he warned, his dark eyebrows drawn together in a worried frown.

She nodded back at him, studying the concern she glimpsed in his steady gaze.

"This wouldn't be the first time he's been up to something, you know," Eric added. He watched her tilt her head slightly to one side with a polite nod of thanks. A few strands of golden hair lay against her cheek, and Eric extended a hand and, with warm fingers, tucked it behind her ear.

Hope stopped thinking, for the moment at least, and enjoyed her husband's tender touch.

Then Eric continued in a faltering voice, "Tell Cassie…I'll try to be there this afternoon, and… Beth, I'll see her at dinner." He watched the warmth in her eyes light with amusement.

"What? No message for Harry?" Hope asked with a sudden curve to one corner of her mouth.

Eric smiled in return. "Tell him I hope he has a nice flight back to Missouri." He breathed in the lovely scent of her perfume before adjusting his tie.

Hope's grin widened. "I think I'll just tell him you said hello."

"Try goodbye instead. He'll get the picture."

Hope's laugh sounded light and gentle. "You probably won't even have to see him, so don't worry about it."

"So, I'm not to dread the impending visit of my least favorite brother-in-law?" Eric asked, still smiling. "Maybe having an hour or two to watch a baseball game tonight would relieve my anxiety about this visit.''

"I'm sure it would help," Hope answered, following Eric to the front door. She placed her hand on the doorknob, leaning her head against the wood as he stepped out onto the porch. "The Reds are playing at 8:00." She'd read it in the paper this morning. They used to watch those games together.

"I'll be here. If everything is okay with the kids, I'm planning to watch at least part of it."

And, maybe, she would join him.

"It's good to see you, Harry." Hope gave her brother a hug as he entered the lobby of the airport to find her waiting there. "I haven't seen you in a while."

"Too long," he agreed, and kissed her cheek. "How are the girls?"

"They're doing well. Beth is at school; Cassie is still in the hospital, but she'll be out soon. Maybe tomorrow, according to her doctor. Come on, let's get your luggage."

The two of them walked to the baggage claim area, catching up on family news on the way. Their parents were both well and thinking about retiring from the bakery they'd owned and operated for the past ten years since they'd moved to Missouri; their younger sister Hannah had recently bought a house close to where her parents lived, and Harry's two sons, who were being raised by their mother, were doing about average in school and enjoying the return of baseball season.

"What about Jeanie? How has she been doing?"

"I'm not like you, Hope. I don't keep tabs on my former spouse. I guess I was ready to let go of the past and get on with my future."

"Jeanie was a friend of mine—of course I'm interested in what happens to her. We all went to school together. And, I might remind you, I don't have a 'former' spouse to keep track of yet, Harry. Eric and I are still married. You know that."

"Too bad for you, sis. I thought maybe you would have moved on by now. You can be sure Eric has."

Hope pulled her hand away from where she had looped it casually through her brother's arm. "What's that supposed to mean?"

Harry laughed and shook his head. "Nothing. Nothing at all. There, that brown suitcase with the black handle is mine." He reached for it as it came along on the conveyor belt.

Hope watched him pick up his luggage. Only one bag. That was good. He couldn't be staying long. How much trouble could he stir up? "Eric is not with someone new, if that's what you were implying. As a matter of fact, he's living with me again." Hope enjoyed the expression of surprise on Harry's face; the simple statement was loaded with more suggestion than truth.

Harry put down his suitcase with a curse. "How

could you let that happen? You were on your way to straightening out your life.''

''Maybe I think being Eric's wife is the best way to straighten out the mess we've made of things.''

Harry's blue eyes flashed at the sister he was instantly angry with. ''You should never have married him,'' he said, picking up the suitcase and walking on. ''Divorcing him would be the best possible thing. Then you could come back to Missouri with me and get your life in order.''

''Missouri?'' This time it was Hope who stopped walking. ''What on earth made you think I'd want to go back with you? My home is here. In Columbus. My kids are in school here. This is my home, Harry. And I love it.''

''But without Eric, you could start over—''

''If I start over, it will be here. Right here with my girls...with or without Eric.''

''Maybe. Maybe not.'' Harry's answer and sudden smile caught Hope off guard, and she frowned back at him.

''What are you talking about?''

''I have a business idea I want to share with you. We'll talk over lunch,'' he explained. ''First, I want to get settled into a room, see the girls—and then we'll discuss it.''

''Harry,'' Hope said with some hesitation. ''You know how things are between you and Eric. It would be better if you're not at the house during your stay—''

"Don't worry. If Eric stays out of my way, I'll stay out of his."

Hope nodded in agreement, but she doubted Harry would live up to his end of this deal. He was her brother, and she loved him, but even she had accepted that his reliability was questionable. "We could have dinner together—"

"Lunch will have to do for today, Hope. I have a meeting this evening with a banker friend of mine who lives here in the city. We are trying to work out an agreement for a loan," Harry explained. "But I could see you and the girls anytime tomorrow."

A banker friend and a loan. As they left the airport in search of a restaurant, Hope was curious about what her brother was up to this time around. Over lunch, she began to learn exactly how he planned to involve her.

When Hope finished her lunch with her brother, she left him so he could take care of the business matters that seemed to consume his thoughts and his time today. That's probably how it would be throughout the visit. She should have listened to Eric, she thought as she drove toward the hospital to visit Cassie. In some ways Eric knew Harry better than she did. Harry wasn't here so much to see Hope and the girls as he was to involve her in a plan to purchase their parents' bakery. Surely, that couldn't be the Lord's will for her. At least, she couldn't imagine He'd want her to move in that direction. Change everything.

Still, although Hope knew she should probably leave alone the whole idea of investing in any of her brother's businesses, she couldn't help but at least play with the idea. A different life in a different place. Baking cookies instead of teaching a class full of rowdy children. Daily interaction with Harry and her parents. Maybe it would give them the time needed to work out the differences they'd had over the years. Or…maybe not, Hope thought with a grimace. It might not improve their relationships at all, and there she'd be—stuck in another city, another state, with her equity money invested in a business she'd want out of. Without Eric.

"It's a treehouse." Eric answered Hope's question while taking a few steps back to view his project. "At least, it's supposed to be. Don't tell me it looks *that* bad."

Hope shook her head as she eyed his creation with curiosity. She had just returned home from lunch with her brother and a visit with Cassie to find Eric, much to her surprise, spending the free time he had that afternoon working on a "secret" project. Her fleeting thought of telling him about Greg Shelton was forgotten.

"No, it probably looks like you meant it to look, I guess," she replied. "It's just—what use do you think your parents are going to have for a treehouse in their backyard at their age?''

Eric laughed and leaned over to retrieve the hammer he had abandoned earlier. ''When Dad said he thought this would be a good idea, I think he had grandchildren in mind. Don't you?'' He glanced back into Hope's troubled expression.

''Well, I hope he was talking about Angela's kids or Rob's. Not ours. I really don't want the girls climbing up that high—''

''It's not so high,'' Eric defended. Glancing toward the structure, he estimated the distance from the small enclosure to the ground. ''Eight feet, maybe? Not much more. The girls will love it. Beth already tried it out when she came home from school. She's in the house now calling Cassie to tell her about it. She's talking about getting curtains for the windows after Cassie comes home.''

''I don't want Beth or Cassie up there.'' She squinted, lifting a hand to shade her eyes from a brief peek of the sun, the first break in the clouds she'd seen all day. ''Neither of them ever mentioned a treehouse to me.''

''Probably because they knew you would react just like this,'' Eric said quietly. ''You're too protective.''

''Too protective,'' Hope repeated, not surprised by his comment. ''After all we've been through with Cassie's injury? Now, trying to protect them from further harm makes me overly protective?''

Hope longed to say more, but guilt kept her from it. The warmth of a blush colored her face, and she looked away from Eric, toward the ground.

Enjoying a treehouse wouldn't be the first activity Hope had kept their children from enjoying over the past year or more. Playing soccer, inline skating, swimming and horseback riding were a few of the pleasures she had denied her daughters since Cassie had made that unfortunate dive. She, herself, knew that, at times, she was overly protective. And she hated saying 'no' to some of their requests almost as much as the kids hated hearing it. But, each and every time an opportunity came up like this for her girls, Hope had felt justified in her decision. And Eric hadn't been around to counter her refusals. Until now.

"I know you love the kids—" Eric paused "—Hope, you've got to let them live a little. You can't protect them from life."

"That's easy for you to say," she retorted. "But you've never—" She stopped speaking, realizing where her words were leading. She didn't want to go there. "You weren't watching when Cassie got hurt," she added in a soft voice. "You don't know how it feels to be so helpless...so responsible."

"You're not responsible for Cassie's accident just because you took the girls swimming on a hot summer afternoon." Eric gathered up a few nails and continued on with the work he was doing, nailing three boards into a makeshift table for the shelter. "I don't know how many times I'll have to tell you that. You didn't push her off the board that day. You're not to blame, so let it go." He had raised his voice loud enough to be heard over the hammering, but lowered it again when he stopped. He looked directly into Hope's liquid blue eyes, which were wide with regret—or sorrow, or something. "Let it go, Hope."

She gave a slight shrug of dismissal. She wished she could let it go, leave her doubts behind, start over. But she couldn't seem to make that kind of progress. Not now, and not with Eric.

"I don't want to cheat them out of their childhood fun, Eric, but I am afraid for them. Broken arms, broken necks...so many things can happen so quickly. The only way to protect them is to prevent them from being in potentially dangerous situations."

Eric's eyes searched her face for a moment. "You've criticized me for leaving the church, but I was just being honest. When I didn't believe anymore, I left. You're still attending, but you've apparently left a lot of God's teachings by the wayside. Sitting on a pew every week isn't going to help you in life if you don't trust the Lord."

Hope frowned. "What does that have to do with a treehouse for the kids?"

"It has something to do with all of life. You were the one who believed God would heal Cassie slowly, through the care of physicians. And, He did. He didn't let you down.''

"I know that,'' Hope countered. "I didn't say He *had* let me down.''

"But some of your actions say that. Don't you think God would want our children to have a happy, healthy, normal childhood? Don't you think He can take care of them whether they're climbing a ladder into a treehouse or inline skating at the mall?''

"Did He take care of Cassie when she dove off that board?'' Hope quietly asked the question she'd not allowed herself to ask anyone before today.

"He didn't perform a miracle and spare her harm—no. But, I think that from the moment of the accident until this moment today, He's been with her, helping her in a variety of ways. Don't you?''

Hope cast a questioning look in her husband's direction. "You're having second thoughts? About God?''

"Maybe.'' Eric's gaze lowered to the ground momentarily as Hope stared at him in waiting silence. Then he looked back into her curious eyes. "I guess anything is possible. Isn't it?''

Hope's mouth curved with a tender smile. "Yes.'' Anything was possible.

"You did nothing wrong in taking the girls swimming that day. That's how I see it, Hope. But if you feel guilty for some reason I can't understand, pray about it. Ask the Lord for His forgiveness or for freedom from this feeling that you've done something wrong." Eric made a sweeping motion with his hand toward the sky. "Don't you think God is capable of granting you that?"

Hope nodded in mute agreement. She was supposed to be the Christian, the "religious" one in this discussion. How this had turned into an "Eric preaching to Hope" scenario eluded her completely. It was certainly a turn of events she wouldn't have predicted. "All right, Eric. I'll try your suggestion. But I'm still not sure about letting the kids use that treehouse."

"Not even if you're with them?"

"Me? In that treehouse?" Hope glanced up at the bare-bones structure that filled up a spacious spot on an old oak tree. "I don't think so, Eric."

A lazy grin played at the corners of his mouth. "Why not? Afraid it won't hold your weight?" he asked.

"Very funny," Hope remarked, giving the pine boards stacked beside her husband a critical glance. "It's the quality of the construction I'm questioning."

Eric's laugh was deep and generous. "Have no concerns about that. Like it or not, you're still married to a man who can do just about whatever he sets his mind to."

That twinkle Hope missed was back in Eric's eyes, and it made her smile, too. "Correction," she replied. "I'm married to a man who *thinks* he can do whatever he sets his mind to. Therein lies the danger."

Chapter Five

"Eric, you need channel ten!" she called from the kitchen when she heard him switch on the wide-screen television later than evening. She'd spent part of the day with Harry and the rest of it with the girls. The fact that her brother had a meeting tonight pleased her more than she'd admit. She needed this time to think about the offer he'd made regarding the purchase of their parents' bakery. Anything financial that involved Harry Ryan made Hope uneasy, and Eric would be angry when he found out that she was even *remotely* considering such an investment with her brother.

Eric had come home only moments earlier. She was excited about telling him that Cassie might be coming home in the morning as her doctor had suggested in their telephone conversation earlier. She *wasn't* excited about telling him about Greg Shelton. But she had to get it out in the open soon, or the girls certainly would.

"Beth, honey, are you coming downstairs?" Hope called.

"Yep," the girl replied as she hurried down the steps, dragging her worn little bear behind her. "Baseball time?"

"Yes," Hope said. "For about half an hour, then it's bedtime."

Beth turned toward the living room and ran straight for the sofa, jumping on the cushion closest to her father.

"Hi, babe." Eric greeted her with a hug. "Gonna watch TV with me?"

"Yep, for a while. Hey, Mom! Aren't you coming?" she called out to her mother, who stood behind them. Hope was watching the back of her little girl's golden head bob around as she made herself comfortable on the large, soft couch with her dark-haired father.

"Yes, I'm coming," Hope replied, then turned to pick up the glasses of ice and soda she had poured for the three of them. "I have good news, guys. There's a chance Cassie could come home tomorrow."

"Yeah!" Beth was shouting and jumping up and down on the sofa cushions as Hope set the tray of drinks on the coffee table.

"When did you find out?" Eric asked.

"A few hours ago. I spoke with Dr. Lewis, and he said she's doing great. He'll decide tomorrow if she can be discharged. She might even be able to go back to school in a week or less."

"And Uncle Harry is here, too! Tomorrow's going to be a great day!" Beth proclaimed.

The look Eric sent Hope was not subtle. His annoyance at the idea of Harry's presence darkened his expression. But what did Eric want her to do? Cut herself off completely from her family?

"Can I skip school tomorrow, please, Mom, since there's so much going on?" Beth begged.

"No, you may not," Hope responded. "Your father and I have a lot to do, and you need to be in school."

"I wish you had told me sooner about Cassie coming home from the hospital. I would have liked to talk to Dr. Lewis about it," Eric said.

Hope frowned. "But he's only letting her come home if she's able, Eric, that's what we've been wanting. She hasn't had a fever for over forty-eight hours."

"Remember what happened the last time? She wasn't home two days when her fever shot back up and she had to be readmitted. That was more upsetting to her than if she'd stayed in the hospital the whole time. I don't want to go through that again." He picked up the remote and located the correct channel; the ball game was just coming on.

"I want her home, but I want her completely well first."

Hope was startled by Eric's manner. He spoke very matter-of-factly. He sounded distant and firm, as though he was giving her the final offer on a piece of property rather than discussing their child. He could be that way too easily sometimes.

"When I go over there later to spend the night with her, maybe I should tell her how pleased her father is that she's coming home tomorrow," Hope said sarcastically. Then she picked up one of the sodas and took a slow drink.

Eric's brown eyes met her cool gaze. "You know exactly what I mean, Hope. Don't make this look like I'm guilty of some crime. I want Cassie home as badly as you do. Especially now that I'm staying here, in the same house she's coming home to—"

Beth interrupted them both. "Game's starting," she said quietly from where she sat in the middle of the couch with her feet tucked up under her. "I can't hear it if you're gonna talk."

Both adults looked at her, almost with a sense of a relief for the intrusion. Maybe that's what their relationship needed, a referee, Hope thought as she sank into the cushions close to Beth. No, she knew exactly what it needed: the love they had known in days gone by...and the ability to forget the past.

So, baseball began that night, and less than two innings into the game, Beth had fallen asleep, leaning against her father's arm.

"I'll carry her upstairs," Eric said, and he did so. Hope went ahead of him and pulled the blanket and sheet down so he could ease their daughter into bed without waking her. Hope gently covered her, tucking the light blue blanket up under her chin.

"She looks like an angel," Eric remarked, touching the fair skin of Beth's cheek. "I told Angela that about Andrea the other day, and she was quick to explain how wrong I was."

Hope laughed quietly. "Catch us in the wrong mood and any mom will argue that point with you. Fathers would, too, if they were the ones raising the kids."

Her remark hurt Eric; she knew it by his silence. He lowered his head a little and, she suspected, held back whatever response he would have liked to give.

"I'm sorry," she said, genuinely regretting her implication. "I didn't mean that you're not involved in raising the girls. I just meant that—"

"That it's mostly you in their lives. Daily. Nightly. Always," he responded. As Eric lifted his gaze to meet hers, Hope saw the sadness that had settled over him. "I know that you're closer to them than I'll ever be."

"They adore you, Eric. Your relationship with them is wonderful. The only way you could improve it is to live with them permanently." *There,* she'd said the unthinkable. But it was true. Raising the kids together, even like this, was preferable to going it alone. If Greg Shelton could consider such a thing, why couldn't Eric? Didn't he think he could learn to love her again?

"I don't want something agreed to for the sake of the children." He wouldn't agree to any "arrangement," he thought. He could barely even discuss the idea. He wanted a real marriage with Hope, and he certainly couldn't go on indefinitely living like this—having her a part of his daily life, but not really having her at all. "Neither one of us would be satisfied with that, Hope."

She nodded, almost speechless at his remark. Didn't he think they could love each other again the way they once had? "You don't think—I mean, given time..." She started speaking and then stopped.

"I don't know," he responded. How long would it take for Hope to open up to him, love him again the way she once had? Eric looked at his sleeping daughter. He and Hope were compatible enough to make an "arrangement" work. But he wanted more. God wouldn't fault him for that, would He?

Hope swallowed the panic that was rising in her throat. How could he feel so hopeless about their relationship? Wasn't what they'd known in the past worth fighting for? But she couldn't say anything more without sobbing, and she wasn't about to let Eric see her cry. Not when he'd been the one who was unfaithful. Come to think of it, he should have been coming to her for forgiveness. That was something he'd never bothered to do.

Then Eric took a necessary risk and brought up the past. "Hope…there are things we need to talk about."

She lowered her gaze to stare at the burgundy carpet of the bedroom and blinked hard, not wanting tears to fall. "Not now," she said quietly before turning to go.

"Hope, please listen—"

"I just can't. Not now, Eric," she replied on her way out the door. She had to leave the room before she sobbed her heart out right there in front of him.

Eric stood there for a moment in Beth's room, considering what to do next. He hadn't meant to hurt Hope. Ever. All he wanted was their life back.

Hope's heart pounded as she rushed down the steps. How could she have thought he might suggest they try again? For the sake of the kids, or otherwise? Whatever spark of optimism that had ignited in her momentarily had been quickly doused. Maybe he didn't want to hurt her again by spelling out how adamant he was about the divorce. They'd be divorced by now if he'd had his way in this matter. She'd been the one who stopped everything by refusing to sign those papers.

Eric started slowly down the stairs behind her, but, when they reached the bottom, Hope went to the right to enter the kitchen while he turned toward the living room. Hope was glad for a few minutes of privacy as she pulled a paper towel from the wooden dispenser to blot up the tears beginning to spill from her eyes. She wanted to be away from everyone and everything. Even if only for a moment. *Divorced.* She'd never thought that would happen to her. To them. If you loved God, lived by the Bible, did things the way things were meant to be done, weren't you supposed to get a happy ending?

"Hope?"

She heard Eric speak her name from beyond the kitchen doorway. She wiped her eyes quickly and stuffed the paper towel with mascara smudges on it into the trash can just as he walked through the door.

"You all right?" he asked, studying her reddened eyes and tight-lipped expression.

"Uh-huh." She nodded and cleared her throat nervously. "I thought—maybe…would you like some popcorn?" she asked suddenly, surprised at her own idea. She reached to open a cupboard over the sink. "I think your mother keeps it up here—"

"Hope—"

"I can't quite reach it," she interrupted.

Eric hesitated. "Here," he said, "I'll get it." He picked up the yellow box that was just beyond Hope's fingertips and handed it to her. "Popcorn sounds good," he said quietly, feeling as though something *should* be said. Something other than how much he missed her tonight, or how he wished she'd really listen to him and let him explain. His dark eyes searched her watery gaze.

"I—I'd better put this in the microwave," Hope said softly, "before I totally forget what I'm doing."

Eric smiled. Maybe she was feeling as awkward as he was. There were times he could read the emotions in her eyes. But not tonight.

"When you finish in here, come watch the rest of the game with me," he suggested. "Cassie's not expecting you at the hospital this early in the evening, is she?"

"No," Hope answered. "I told her I'd be there around ten o'clock. Trudy's working again tonight, so she'll be fine until then."

Eric watched her movements as she cut open the cellophane wrapper and put the sack of popcorn into the oven. Maybe he should wait until another day to talk to her; maybe he should go into the living room and wait for her to join him. He'd probably make her nervous standing there, leaning back against the counter, watching her, as he was doing. But he couldn't seem to leave. Through most of their relationship he'd enjoyed helping her do simple tasks in the kitchen. It had often provided them with romantic moments alone, with the kids not underfoot.

"Would you get the bowl in the dish rack? I'll put the popcorn in it," Hope said as she pulled the hot snack from the oven. When she tugged on the corners of the bag to let the steam out, she failed to move her hand quickly enough, and some of the steam burned her fingers. "Ouch!" she exclaimed, jerking her hand away from the heat and letting the bag fall over and the popcorn spill out onto the counter. She turned and reached for the cold water faucet just as Eric did the same.

"You okay?" he asked, switching on the flow of cold water and letting it run over her reddened fingers.

"Yes, it's all right," she said. "What a stupid thing to do. You'd think I'd never opened a bag of hot popcorn in my life."

Eric took Hope's hand in his own, looking over the injury. "I know it hurts, but I think you'll live," he remarked, one corner of his mouth curving up in a half smile that held steady even when he met her gaze. Then it occurred to him that she'd made no effort to retrieve her hand.

Hope swallowed at the lingering lump in her throat. Eric's eyes seemed darker, more solemn than she'd ever seen them. Her fingers stung slightly, but the soothing stroke of his thumb against the back of her hand made up for the hurt she'd suffered.

"The water—" she said quickly, glancing toward the faucet they'd left running.

Her words broke the look they were both nearly lost in, and Eric reached to turn the tap off, still not releasing her hand. He picked up a dish towel and

far as she could recall. No, Eric was a wonderful father. And that knowledge only served to make Hope feel guiltier than ever about her own mistakes.

Eric went on. "Remember how it was in those days? We were consumed with worry about Cassie." He rubbed a hand down his face in exasperation. "I don't know how we got through it."

"With God's help, that's how we did it. One day at a time until Cassie was well," Hope stated. She remembered the refuge she had taken in prayer during those days. And the Bible verses she'd clung to. Without the Lord, she knew she'd never have made it.

"You're right. I should have been thankful for what we had," he agreed. "But through all of that, I kept thinking God would heal Cassie. Instantaneously, I mean. I knew He could if He chose to, and I just didn't see why He wouldn't choose to. And then, that scripture about all things working together for our good." He paused, sliding a hand into the pocket of his dark slacks as he considered the gravity of his admission. He'd doubted God. Anyway he analyzed it, that was what it amounted to. "I didn't see anything good coming out of Cassie's accident. Nothing. And, you—" he shook his head slightly "—I lost you completely."

Hope's eyes filled with tears. "But just about the time Cassie improved, you gave up on God's help. If you hadn't done that—"

"No, it wasn't that," he interrupted. "I shouldn't have blamed God, I know. I guess He was just an easy target." Eric paused. "But I'd lost you long before then." He watched the corners of Hope's mouth take a sad turn downward, but she didn't deny the truth of his words. "Why, Hope? What happened with us?"

Hope released her hold on the counter and folded her hands together in front of her in some pretense of composure. "I don't know."

A frown settled over his dark features. She *did* know. He could see it in her actions, the way she wouldn't meet his gaze just now. The longing they'd felt for each other such a short time ago, though very real, hadn't moved them a single step closer to honesty. And Eric knew honesty was what they needed if they were to find their way back to each other.

Then for the first time, a thought crossed his mind—a thought he didn't like. Maybe she felt guilty about something. Or someone. Maybe that had been the source of the distance between them. And he remembered the principal Cassie and Hope had both mentioned. Surely, it couldn't be that. "Did you know Greg Shelton before you started teaching at Beechwood?"

Hope's eyes widened in surprise at his question. "Greg Shelton? He has nothing to do with us—"

"You didn't answer my question," Eric interrupted.

"Yes," she said quickly, a flash of regret flickering through her lovely blue eyes. "He was the assistant principal when I subbed at Elmwood." She hesitated. "Eric, there's nothing between Greg Shelton and me." Nothing, except an offer of marriage, she thought frantically. How was she going to explain that to her husband?

A melancholy frown settled over his expression. He had thought her answer would be "no." Now, where did he go from here? Then he remembered his daughter's words. "Cassie tells me that Mr. Shelton has been discussing the future with you."

Hope's feet felt glued to the floor. She wasn't going to escape this, and she knew she should have told Eric right from the beginning about Greg's statements that day at the lunch table. Why hadn't she? "Cassie has heard me talking about him. Greg is a widower with young children, and…he wants to remarry. He needs someone."

Eric stared at her, momentarily speechless at the implications. "And you are that someone?"

"No—well, not exactly," she stammered. "Eric, this is more complicated than it sounds on the surface. There's nothing between Greg Shelton and me. Nothing more than a casual friendship, but—" She stopped and sighed. He had to be told. "But he did make it known to me, recently, that if I were free…he was interested."

Eric's mouth thinned into a straight line as a darkness stole over his features. "I see," he said.

He almost asked if she wanted to be free, but decided against it. It was obvious his thoughts had been accurate. He'd lost her, maybe long before he'd even become aware of it. And where did her relationship with God fit into all of this?

"Eric, I need to explain this to you. Greg made that offer to me at the lunch table in the cafeteria in front of half a dozen other people. There was nothing touching or romantic about it. We don't have that kind of relationship."

"What kind of a relationship *do* you have with him, Hope?" he asked, his voice cold and distant. He could hardly believe he was having this conversation with her. His wife. The woman whom, a short time ago, he'd thought he might still have a future with. Now, it seemed, she had a different future mapped out for herself.

"We work together, Eric. He's a nice man who wants to provide a better life for his kids than they have now with baby-sitters and day care. He probably thinks of me as someone who could give them that."

But Eric's frown indicated his doubt. "There are plenty of women out there, Hope, *unmarried* women who would be more than happy to help him out of his predicament. Some of them were probably sitting at that lunch table when he made his offer. But he chose you."

Hope dropped her gaze from his. He was right. Her friend, Marcia, and two other young women

eating lunch with her that day were available and
more than a little interested in the principal. But the
offer had been made to Hope.

"If Greg feels anything for me, Eric, it's one-
sided. I've never thought of him in that way, and
I've never done anything to lead him to think I'm
interested."

Eric nodded a little, then glanced toward the
nearby window. Where did they go from here?
Maybe he should ask her. Or maybe he needed to
ask God. At this point, without His help, it didn't
look like *they* would be going anywhere. Rather,
Eric would go his way, and Hope would go hers—
with the kids caught somewhere in the middle. It
surprised him how much it hurt all over again to
face that truth.

"Eric, please, listen to me," Hope pleaded. "I'm
the one who refused to sign the papers for the divorce. Do you think I'd have done that if I wanted
a relationship with Greg Shelton?"

Eric shook his head. "I don't know. I'm not sure
what to think right now, Hope."

"I'm not interested in anyone else. I'm married
to you, I have children with you."

"You and I both love the girls enough to sacri-
fice for them," Eric agreed. "But I don't want them
to be the only reason we are husband and wife. And
I think at the time we separated, they were the only
thing holding us together."

Maybe, back then, that was true, Hope thought.

She swallowed hard. It was difficult to remember. But now...she wanted Eric. His love. Not just his participation in the raising of their girls. But still, if that's all she could have, she'd take it. They could start there; it would lead to more if he allowed it to do so. "Eric, for me, the children would be reason enough," she answered. Should she admit that she loved him? If she did, would she have to tell him what a neglectful parent she had been to their daughter that day at the pool? Was anything worth that?

Eric studied his wife's wary expression. Only minutes ago, he could have sworn it was the woman he'd married that he had in his arms. But now she was gone again, hidden behind that cautious look in Hope's eyes. Eric gave a long sigh as he looked away from her. The clock beside the refrigerator caught his attention: ten o'clock. Cassie would be waiting. He looked back at Hope. "Do you want me to go to the hospital? You could stay here with Beth."

Hope shook her head. "I'll go. She's expecting me." She turned and started through the doorway, wiping a stray tear from her face as she moved. Nothing was resolved. It couldn't be, at least not without paying the high price of the truth.

"Hope," he called after her, not wanting to let her go.

She glanced back over her shoulder, suppressing a sob.

"I'm not sorry about kissing you." His solemn gaze startled her; it was so dark, so desolate. "It's what we both wanted."

Hope gave a slight nod, but she didn't respond. She couldn't, not without telling him that was only the beginning of what she wanted from him—a lifetime together.

Chapter Six

Eric stood on the porch with his arms full of morning mail and about a dozen thick manila folders. He was just about to leave for the office, when he saw Hope mowing the patch of grass in front of the flower bed. "Have you been to the hospital already?"

She'd seen Eric's mouth move but couldn't hear his question over the sound of the engine, so she shut it off. "I'm sorry. I couldn't hear you. What did you say?"

"Did you go to the hospital?" he asked.

"About an hour ago. Dr. Lewis hasn't been in to see Cassie yet this morning, so I'll check later about her being discharged today." She brushed some grass off her ankles. "How's your mom? Have you talked to your father?"

"Yes. She's doing very well. Much better than expected."

Eric descended the porch steps and walked up to where Hope was standing by the tulips. Red, yellow, purple, white—the colors were impossible to ignore. Eric was reminded of the countless varieties of flowers Hope had planted around the old Victorian home they had owned together. He'd driven out of his way to see the slate-blue house the other day, only to find it was now an odd shade of green. And the new owners had torn out most of the landscaping that he and Hope had spent hours perfecting. Plants, shrubs, even the fragrant lilac bushes in various shades of lavender across the back of the property were gone. Nothing was the same anymore. Not even that simple piece of real estate—

Eric suddenly remembered the topic they'd been discussing: his mother. "Dad's planning to bring her home soon, so I won't need to fly down there."

"Oh, that's good," Hope said with a sigh of relief, then considered how her words may have sounded. "Good about your mother feeling better, I mean."

Eric studied her unreadable expression momentarily, then averted his gaze to the mower. "Yard work is not your responsibility, Hope. If the kid next door can't do this, I'll take care of it tonight."

Hope shrugged. "He said he could mow, just like always, but I gave him the week off so I could do it instead." She tipped her face up toward the sun, enjoying its warmth. "I haven't mowed a lawn since we sold our house, Eric. I want to do this to have an excuse to be outside."

"You could sit on the porch and watch the cars go by, you know. You don't need an excuse to be outdoors."

"You don't, but I do," she countered. "With me, there's always something else I could be doing *inside*." She smiled. "Sometimes I'm inside so much it makes me a little crazy. I guess mowing is kind of like my therapy for the week."

Eric shook his head. "And what will it be next week? Roof repair? Dad said that's the next project to be done."

"I don't love spring weather *that* much," she said with a soft laugh. "Anyway, if I did the roofing, we'd probably have more leaks after the work than before I started."

"I doubt it," Eric remarked with a twinge of sadness. "You've always been good at whatever you set your mind to."

Hope pushed back hair that was slipping out of her haphazard ponytail. "Everything except keeping a marriage together?"

"That's not all your fault, you know," Eric told her. His expressionless face offered no hint of emotion. "It was my marriage, too."

"It still is," she shot back. Or at least, it could be, she thought.

But the marriage he longed for was the loving

one they used to enjoy. And that was nothing like the arrangement they had now—an arrangement with which Hope seemed content. So Eric did not agree or disagree with her remark. He merely studied the silent slant of her mouth a moment longer than Hope could endure.

"You were on your way to work, weren't you?" she asked in a tense, clipped voice. How many times would she make open-ended statements that this man would disregard? It *was* still his marriage, too.

"Yes, work." He looked away from her, toward the driveway that held both their vehicles. "I'll be there most of the day." He paused. "My lawyer would like to talk to us, again—together." He looked back into her wide blue eyes. "But I told him 'no.'"

"Thank you," she answered. Then Hope's hands wrapped around the handle of the mower. Lowering her eyes, she stared down at her grass-stained tennis shoes. "Until Cassie's home again, I don't even want to think about legal matters."

"I agree," Eric responded.

"But, then—" Hope stopped speaking, wondering briefly if she had the courage to continue her thought out loud. She decided she did, since she didn't have much left to lose. "But then, if you would want to…maybe we could try talking to Rob."

"He's not practicing law anymore, Hope. We don't need Rob's input on this matter—"

"I don't mean as a lawyer. I mean...as a counselor."

Eric frowned.

"He does marriage counseling. He's a pastor, Eric. We're the kind of people he deals with. Maybe he could help—"

"Hope, I love my brother. But that's what Rob is to me. My brother. And I'm not going to discuss intimate details of my life with him." He spoke adamantly, leaving no room for negotiation. Hope could hear it in his tone, see it in the determined set of his jaw.

She nodded. In some ways, she understood. "Then...a different counselor maybe?" she asked.

"That's a possibility," Eric answered. "If we could find the right one."

Hope nodded. Then she pulled on the mower cord, hard and quick, but the engine on the mower didn't fire.

"I'll get it for you," Eric offered, but before he could empty his arms of folders and mail, Hope refused his help.

"I can do this," she insisted. The color rose in her cheeks and she felt her face warm. "I started it by myself earlier." She yanked harder once more, and was thankful when the engine started. "Thanks, anyway."

Eric nodded, feeling oddly discouraged. He

would have liked to help her. But then, what had he expected? Hope was never the helpless-female type. Not from her earliest days. "I've gotta go," he said after taking a quick glance at his watch. He leaned close so she could hear his words over the mower's engine. "The receptionist will be there waiting on me. She doesn't have a key."

Hope looked quickly down at the tulips. She didn't feel like talking about his office help. Then she thought of his words last night. They were words she believed.

"You'd like Mrs. Kendell," Eric added, drawing Hope's blue gaze back up to meet his own. "She reminds me of my mother."

"Sounds charming," she replied loudly over the roar of the engine. She would have liked to smile when she said it, but couldn't find it in herself to do so. "I've never known you to be interested in older women."

"I like one the same age as I am. That's worked just fine for me. Until recently," he added. Leaning close to be heard left Eric near enough to notice how wonderful Hope smelled: light perfume, fresh-cut grass.

Hope gave a small smile when she thought of his last remark. She was Eric's age—almost exactly, since they both celebrated mid-October birthdays. Last fall had been the first time they'd not observed the occasions together.

He nodded a silent goodbye and, with difficulty,

turned away from her. It would have been easy to kiss her again, right there, in the front yard, in front of God and whoever else was looking. But he didn't.

As she watched him walk toward the truck in the driveway, she whispered a prayer she'd repeated countless times, for Eric to get his heart right with God. That was the new starting point he needed—*they* needed. And the next prayer should be for herself, she knew. The Lord could help her say what she needed to say, and somehow protect Cassie's heart while she did so. She shut off the mower, pushed it to the side and headed toward the house as tears began to slip down her cheeks. She'd been a Christian long enough to know where she needed to turn. Her Heavenly Father. The Lord would have to lead them back to each other.

"Hello, Harry. How are you?" Eric extended his hand for a necessary handshake with his brother-in-law as he greeted him later that day in the large entryway of the Granston house. Eric had stopped at home to pick up some paperwork he'd forgotten to take with him that morning and found Harry there, waiting for Hope.

"Hi, Eric. I'm kinda surprised to see you. I thought you'd be out of the picture by now."

Harry's smirk irritated Eric. Eric knew Harry could see the flash of anger in his dark eyes. But Eric had already determined to try to get through this with the least friction possible, so when he responded to the remark, his tone sounded relatively civil.

"Yep, still here." Eric's mouth twisted in a wry smile. He glanced around the room casually. "The setting has changed, and the script...but Hope and I are still married—much to your dismay, I'm sure."

Harry nodded. "Well, maybe I can speed things up for you. I'm trying to talk Hope into going back to Missouri with me."

Eric studied Harry's expression. His brother-in-law appeared to be rather pleased with himself, and Eric couldn't help but wonder why, considering the man's track record in life. "Hope is happy here, Harry. She has no reason to move away."

"Mother and Dad are retiring from the bakery. If I can convince Hope to become partners with me, we could take it over. Business is very good now. It would be more money for her, she could be her own boss and she'd be close to her family." Harry adjusted the red-print tie that clearly clashed with the brown suit he wore.

Eric shook his head. "She wouldn't make a move like that. She's been happier here, away from her parents, than she ever was with them. Her family is right here."

"Not for long. When she's free of you, she's free of the Granstons. And if you ask me, a divorce

seems like a small price to pay for that liberation."
Then he smiled.

With temper flaring into white-hot anger, Eric
turned his head to the side a little, looking away
and biting back words that longed to be said. Then
he gave up the battle and looked back at his
brother-in-law. "Harry, get out of this house. If
Hope wants to spend time with you, it's going to
be somewhere else. Not here, around me."

Harry was quick to counter Eric's demand. "You
can't throw me out of here. Hope is my sister."

"That's not her fault. Fate dealt her that blow,"
Eric remarked, and turned to pull open the heavy
wood door for the Harry's departure.

"I'm not going anywhere, Eric. You don't even
own this house—"

"Harry, please leave." Hope's voice came from
behind the two men. They both looked up as she
came down the staircase from the second floor, her
face nearly as white as the silky blouse she wore.
"I'll call you later at the hotel."

Harry's glare collided with Eric's fiery gaze, then
Harry turned to go.

Eric watched him walk out of the house toward
a rental car parked in the driveway. Then Eric
pushed the door shut with a short-lived sense of
satisfaction. Sliding his hands into the pockets of
his slacks in a resigned manner, he lowered his head
and took a deep breath before he turned to confront
Hope's indignation. He'd been rude to her brother

and, whatever his reasons, she wouldn't be pleased with him. He raised his eyes to hers, expecting to find disdain, but was surprised to find something else.

"He's right, you know," Hope said. Something very near despair shadowed her fair features. "Your family belongs to you. Not me."

"Harry's never been right about anything in his life, and you know it," Eric snapped, disliking the sadness he'd found in those lovely blue eyes. "My parents love you. My whole family loves you."

All of them except you. Hope nearly said the words. They were right there, ready to leap from her heart, but she held them back. "Still, my family is in Missouri. Maybe the girls and I should go there."

"No," Eric said suddenly. "You can't."

Hope had reached the bottom step by now, and she was only a few feet from him. "I can if I want to," she replied simply.

"But I don't want you to go," he admitted. "Your family won't be as good to you as mine will, and the girls should be here, close to me and my parents."

Hope searched his dark eyes, wanting something more than the words he was saying. "Harry thinks we should buy the bakery. My parents have done very well with it these past few years. It might be a wise investment."

Eric sensed something that didn't add up right.

How could his brother-in-law have enough money to buy into a business like that? Eric and Hope had bailed him out of trouble for writing bad checks at least twice during their marriage, and the family bakery wasn't a small mom-and-pop operation that would sell cheaply. It supplied baked goods to most of the major restaurants in the city. "Are your parents letting Harry have his half for free? How could he have that kind of money, Hope? He hasn't had a decent job in years, and he should still be paying child support to his former wife for the boys."

Hope looked down at the moss-green carpeting at her feet. Here was the part she dreaded revealing. "We could use my equity from the sale of our house as a down payment on it." She paused, her mind filled with arguments against making such a purchase. But she didn't like giving up so easily on the idea. After all, it did offer another option for her and the girls.

Eric waved a hand in the air in frustration. "You are far too intelligent to get caught up in one of Harry's schemes. I realize you don't value my opinion much anymore, but *don't* listen to Harry. Go with your own instincts on this, Hope. Don't let him waste your money."

"I'll be careful," she responded. "I haven't decided one way or the other yet."

"Talk to Dad or Mom, Rob or Adam—or someone else whose opinion you trust," he suggested with a shrug. "None of them would approve of this deal. Not one of them." He raked a hand through his dark hair as he hesitated. "Don't do this, Hope. Don't take the girls five-hundred miles away from me, and waste all your equity in the process."

Hope raised her teary eyes to meet his dark frown of concern. He had reasons for his adamant words, but none was the reason Hope was looking for. "I won't do anything hastily. And whatever I do, I'll discuss it with your parents first."

Eric nodded, appearing satisfied with her answer. In reality, he wasn't. He didn't want her to go. He wanted her right here with him. Always. In every way. But it wouldn't happen until they reached the truth. And they weren't there yet. There had to be something she wasn't telling him. He glanced at the clock on the wall behind her; he was late for an appointment.

"I guess your relationship with my brother hasn't changed much," Hope said, interrupting his troubled thoughts.

"I should apologize to you for throwing Harry out," Eric said, then grinned a little. "I think it was just something I'd always wanted to do."

Hope couldn't resist smiling back. "A fantasy come true," she commented, shaking her head as she walked past him toward the kitchen. "You're terrible, Eric Granston," she added. And sometimes he was. But she loved him anyway.

Hope pulled the cord of the draperies, opening them to brighten her brother's hotel room. "Harry?

Why do you keep it so dreary in here? You've got to let a little light in.''

Harry glanced up from the briefcase he was digging through. "Yeah, okay, whatever," he replied, rustling papers and obviously distracted by his thoughts. "Are you ready to go over these figures?"

"You mean, about the bakery? Again?" Hope asked needlessly. The purchase of their parents' bakery had dominated Harry's conversation since he'd arrived, taking precedence over all other subjects, including his nieces. The deal was evidently the reason he had made this trip, rather than to visit family, as Hope had wanted. Eric had been right about Harry's intentions all along.

"C'mon, Hope. Don't act like you don't know what I'm talking about. This is important to me."

"I'd like to think that, in some regard, *I'm* important to you. You didn't come here to see me or my kids, Harry. You're just here to sell me on an idea, and I'm not buying. Leave me out of this bakery deal. I don't want to be involved in it," she said. "All you want to talk about is this silly business deal you've conjured up—"

"Believe me, Hope, there's nothing silly about it. We could get rich with this. Just give this a listen and you'll see—it makes too much sense to turn down. A little money is all you need."

A little money. Hope shook her head in frustration. "Eric warned me—"

"Eric?" Harry retorted. "What does he have to do with this? He's part of your past, Hope. Do you really think Eric wants to see you do well? His recommendations will be exactly the opposite of what you should do with your life."

"That's not true." Hope brushed a few stray hairs away from her eyes. "Eric wouldn't intentionally steer me in the wrong direction. Unlike you, who are only interested in pointing me in the way you want me to go—or perhaps I should say, the way you want my money to go."

Harry laughed. "You're funny, Hope. I'm your blood relative, and you think I'd take advantage of you, but Eric, a man who is anxious to be free of you and the life you've shared for years—*he* is the one you listen to. He stands to gain nothing from this but watching his former wife succeed financially, on her own, and you think that—what?— he'd be happy about that?" Harry sat down, sinking comfortably into an overstuffed chair. "You still haven't wised up, yet, have you, sis?" He reached toward the nearby ashtray and retrieved a cigarette he'd left burning. "Your infatuation with Eric Granston will be your undoing."

"It's not infatuation," Hope answered. "There's nothing foolish or shallow about my feelings for him."

"Not infatuation?" Harry repeated, then shook

his head. "Don't pride yourself on your ability to love. Falling in love is easy. It's the staying part that takes its toll. And neither you nor Eric have mastered that. Have you signed the agreement his lawyer drew up yet?"

"No," Hope replied with a brief shake of her head. Then frowned. "What business is it of yours, anyway?"

Harry chuckled. "None. I just wanted to see if you're making progress, and apparently you are not." Harry paused, then motioned for Hope to have a seat across from him.

"No, thanks. I won't be staying long."

"That's all right, but come back tonight. Our other partner in this deal is Ken Myers. He's with First Choice Banks, which has a branch back home. Remember him? He and I went to college together."

"For one semester," Hope remarked, hugging her blue sweater close. Was it the air conditioning, or just the cool tactics of her brother that sent a shiver down her spine? And what about First Choice Banks? That was the financial institution Hope and Eric had used for the last decade or so. Had Harry known that? She sighed. Harry had talked her into some crazy shenanigans when they were kids—stunts that had gotten them hurt occasionally, and into trouble with their parents frequently. But those days were long gone. He had no sway over her now, no matter how determined he could be. "If Ken is your financial advisor," she offered, "I hope he invested more time in his own education than you did in yours."

"He did. Ken's sharp. I've already talked with him several times about this deal. He wants to meet with you to get your perspective on what we could do with the business."

"I don't want anything to do with the business, Harry. Let Mom and Dad sell it or handle it however they want—"

"They want you in on this." Harry crushed his cigarette in the green glass ashtray by his elbow. "They want you in Missouri with them. That's what I came here for."

"You couldn't just come to see your sister or your nieces?" Hope slid her hands into the deep pockets of her bulky cardigan. "Mom and Dad had no idea whether or not I'd want in on this. They didn't even mention it the last time I spoke with them on the phone. What would make them think I'd want to own that bakery? I didn't show any interest in it in all the years they operated it." Hope raised her hands in an empty gesture. "What made Mom, Dad or you think I'd have the funds to even *consider* buying in to this deal?"

Harry stood up. "You could afford it, if you chose to. That grand old Victorian home you and Eric sold earlier this year wouldn't have gone cheaply. Don't tell me you don't have enough money to invest—"

"So, Eric was right," Hope interrupted, her mouth clamping shut in a frown. She'd tried to ignore the truth, but now it was right out there in the open. Her share of the equity in the sale of her house was what had drawn Harry here now. She had the money to either make this deal fly or take a nosedive. And her brother knew it. "The money that I have is for a down payment on our next house. When the girls and I find the right one—"

"Buy into this bakery, and a year from now you and the girls can buy two or three houses." Harry's eyes narrowed as he shook his head. "You don't know how good a deal this could be, Hope. You don't understand the profits to be made."

"I don't care—"

Harry raised a hand. "Don't say any more until you hear what Ken has to say tonight. He'll be here at 7:00 p.m., sharp. Come then, hear him out. Make your decision after you've listened to Ken."

"I don't want in on this," Hope reiterated as she headed for the door of the hotel room. "I'm not interested, I can't afford it and I don't want to move—"

"—away from Eric," Harry finished with an annoying chuckle. "That's the bottom line, isn't it? It's not the money or the idea of running a bakery that worries you. You just can't leave Eric. I mean, *really* leave him."

"This might not mean much to you, but Eric and

I made promises to each other. I don't think the Lord takes things like that as lightly as you do.''

"So, you're saying—what? That God wants your marriage to survive? And you want to do what He approves of?'' His mouth curved into a bitter smile. "Don't give me that line, little sister.''

"Don't be condescending with me, Harry,'' Hope warned as anger warmed her face. "I'm not twelve years old anymore.''

"No, you're older, but none the wiser, one could assume,'' Harry answered. "At least as far as Granston is concerned. It's not because of God that you want your marriage to hold together. It's not even for your kids. The only reason you want to stay near Granston is because he is what you want, he is all you want in this life. It was always that way.''

It wasn't, was it? "What's the difference? This is none of your business,'' Hope shot back, suddenly uncertain of her own motives.

Harry shrugged, then ran a hand across his mouth in a thoughtful gesture. "Do you think he'd do the same for you? If he had custody of the kids, I mean? Would he let an opportunity this good slip by him just so he could keep the girls close to you—so *he* could stay close to *you?*'' Her brother's eyebrows raised in question.

Hope was speechless. She'd not considered that before now. Would he? she wondered.

"The answer is 'no,''' Harry stated flatly. "He wouldn't.'' He shook his head as if to emphasize the facts as he saw them. "Seven o'clock, Hope. Hear Ken's ideas. Then give me your answer. If you're still not interested, I'll accept that."

Hope pulled open the door and stepped out into the hotel hallway. She shut the door and just stood there for a moment, still reeling from the questions Harry had asked. Would Eric stay close, if he had the girls? It hadn't crossed her mind that he wouldn't do so. They might have almost given up on their marriage, but certainly they hadn't lost all concern for one another's happiness. Or for the girls' feelings. Had they?

Pulling her sweater close around her, she took the elevator down to the parking level and headed toward her van, thinking all the way about the man she'd married. Harry's statement was on target, whether she liked it or not. She didn't want to move away from Eric, to be where she wouldn't run into him, wouldn't have a conversation with him over anything other than their children. He was too much a part of her to let it all end. Eric had remarked that Harry had never been right about anything in his life, but Hope suddenly realized Harry had been very right about at least one thing: her deep feelings for her husband. She didn't want to move away. She didn't want to leave Eric.

Starting the car engine, she backed out and headed toward the exit. She wanted out of this eerie parking garage, out of Harry's business schemes— and away from the truth. Although she knew wanting God's will in her life had been her prayer for many years, it could also be a perfect excuse for pursuing her own desires. Namely, life with Eric.

The glare of the afternoon sunlight was intense as Hope left behind the shadows of the garage for the busy streets of the city. If she was to beat the rush hour, she would need to pick up the groceries she needed now and head straight home, instead of acting on an impulse to take a drive past their old house in the northern part of the county—the old Victorian home that had generated the money Harry had his eyes set on. Hope glanced at her watch. She loved that old house. Maybe the rush-hour traffic wouldn't be that bad.

"Angela?" Hope nearly dropped the bags of groceries from her arms as she entered the Granston kitchen more than an hour later and saw her sister-in-law seated at the breakfast counter with her head down and face buried in her arms, weeping. Hope's heart lurched in panic. "What's wrong? What's happened?"

Angela gave an answer, but it was too muffled to understand. Hope set the bags on the floor, then went immediately to Angela's side and placed a hand on her long dark hair. "Is it your mother? Is she worse?"

Angela lifted her head to look at Hope. "No, no. It's nothing like that."

Then suddenly Hope knew: the adoption plans.

That was what Angela had been so focused on lately. Her heart had been set on proceeding, if only her late-husband's parents would consent to it. "Did you hear from the grandparents?"

Angela's head bobbed up and down in silent, sorrowful affirmation.

"And they said—"

"'No,'" Angela confirmed, shaking her head in reply. "They said, 'no.' Just like that. Without further discussion." Angela paused to wipe her eyes.

Hope watched her sad, strained expression and thought of how rarely she'd seen her sister-in-law exhibit anything other than a youthful happiness. But there was no sign of that today. Hope pushed a box of tissues toward Angela, who gratefully took a few. Then Hope sighed and raised a hand to her own forehead, rubbing the temple where a headache was pounding. "I'm so sorry, Angela. I know how much this means to you and Adam."

"And the kids. Especially, Nathan. He'll be devastated."

"Have you told them yet?" Hope asked, sinking down on the seat beside Angela.

"Just Adam. He's disappointed but not surprised." Angela shrugged. "He's at home right now. Eric is there, too. I needed to get out for a while, so I came over here looking for a shoulder to cry on."

"Well, my shoulder is right here," Hope offered, tilting her head; her smile was bittersweet.

"I know." Angela nodded.

"So, how are you going to tell Nathan?" Hope shivered suddenly at the thought. It was news she wouldn't want to have to tell the boy. It would break his heart.

"I haven't figured that out yet." Angela's face looked pale, miserable. "I'll just...tell him the facts. There's no way to soften the blow."

"I suppose not." Hope settled back in her seat. "The Lord really knew what He was doing when He matched you up with Adam Dalton. He's been a true godsend for you and your children."

Angela nodded. "I guess that's what makes it so hard to accept this news. The kids really want to 'belong' to Adam, and we'd all like to be one big, happy family, rather than a household that is half Sanders and half Dalton."

"Hmm, I'd not thought about that," Hope admitted. "But, remind the kids that in your hearts you are all one loving family—no matter how the birth certificates read."

"I'll try." Angela sniffed again and stood up, pushing a handful of dark hair over her shoulder. "But, somehow, I don't think that's going to be much comfort to Nathan."

"Probably not," Hope responded with increasing sadness. "You know, you could move forward without the grandparents' permission. You could ask Rob about it. Have you thought of that?"

Angela shook her head. "No, I decided when I

asked them their opinion that I would respect their wishes. And I will. Whatever else in this life Dan was, he was the children's father. If the Sanders want their son's name to live on after him, I guess it would have to be through my kids—whether I like it or not."

Hope stood up, too. "Do you want to pray about this?"

Her sister-in-law shook her head again. "Not right now. I know it's probably the best thing to do because prayer changes things, but…the thing that most likely needs to be changed here is my attitude." She offered a smile. "And I'm not ready to let go of that just yet." She leaned forward to give Hope another hug. "I need to go home and explain this to Nathan. I'll see you later."

Hope nodded and folded her arms in front of her as she accompanied Angela to the front door. "Let me know how it goes," she called as she watched Angela head toward the van parked in the driveway. Thinking of how close Nathan and his mother were, she whispered a brief prayer for them. The Lord could help them through this disappointment. He could soothe troubled spirits, mend broken hearts. Many times, He was the only one who could.

Hope reflected for a moment on what Angela had said about not wanting to pray. She knew exactly what her sister-in-law meant. Angela was angry at the Sanders for not agreeing to Adam's adoption of the kids, and, for now at least, she *wanted* to be angry. But eventually Angela would have to let go and let God take care of it.

Hope thought of how tightly she herself had held on to her memories of that day at the pool, when all she needed was to let go and let God take care of it. Completely. She glanced toward the top of the microwave to see the red leather cover of her Bible, right where she'd left it that morning. The "sword of the Lord," her daughters called it with humor and affection after once hearing Grandpa Granston refer to it that way. In a heartfelt moment, Hope blinked back tears and picked up her Bible, opening to the place she kept her bookmark: "Commit thy way unto the Lord, Psalm 37:5a." Hope read the scripture reference and verse aloud to herself where she stood there in the kitchen.

"Maybe I've been wrong," she whispered, more to the Lord than to herself. "Maybe I've not committed my way completely to You. Maybe I've not done all You want me to do. How do I know where I'm headed? And what good will that knowledge do me if You're not leading the way?"

"So, Grace is going into the hospital when she gets home, and Cassie is getting out," Adam said. "One down, one to go."

"Something like that," Eric answered. "We'll find out later today about Cassie. I was just with her at the hospital a while ago, and the doctor hadn't made his rounds yet today." He pulled a bench from the far end of the garage and sat down close to where Adam was cleaning some tools.

"What a day," Adam remarked with a shake of his head. "I feel badly for Angela. She thought she should talk to Nathan alone to explain about the adoption plans falling through."

Just then, the door from the kitchen into the garage flew open, and out came Nathan with his head down and his hands sunk low in the pockets of his faded jeans.

"I'll go so you two can talk privately," Eric said, and turned to leave. This matter was between Adam and Nathan, and Eric left despite their encouragement for him to stay.

But his departing smile was a forced one. Eric was thinking of Adam and Nathan, and how wonderful stepfathers can be. He had never considered being so easily replaced. Dan Sanders had been—that was obvious. Eric had not even considered the possibility of sharing parental privileges with some "wonderful" stepfather whom his own children might someday find themselves loving.

As Eric left Angela and Adam's home that warm May afternoon, Angela came running out the front door after him.

"Eric, wait!" she called.

He looked back at his sister. "Did I forget something?"

"No...Eric, has Hope told you about that day at the pool?"

"Sure she has." She had, hadn't she? Suddenly, he couldn't remember. "Why? What are you getting at?"

"Nothing—maybe." Her reply piqued Eric's curiosity even more. "It's just that..."

"Just what?" he asked.

"I'm no expert on relationships, Eric. Lord knows, my first marriage was a disaster from beginning to end. But if you and Hope want to put your lives back together again, I think you need to have a heart-to-heart talk."

"About Cassie's accident?" he questioned her quietly. "Why? What is there to know?"

Angela shook her head. "Maybe, nothing. But I get the feeling that you haven't heard all the details."

"Cassie decided to dive, went off the board badly and bumped her back on the way down. Is there more to understand than that?"

Angela looked over at Andrea as the little girl came running across the yard. Then she returned her gaze to her brother. "Yes, Eric. There is. But the rest will have to come from Hope."

"Angela..." Eric said, but she turned to scoop Andrea up in her arms and head back toward the house.

"That's all I can tell you. The rest will have to come from Hope," she repeated.

And Eric watched her walk away with some secret she was keeping that didn't belong to her. One that belonged to Hope, and should have been shared with Eric a long time ago. He wondered how he could persuade Hope to confide in him now. Did he have any chance of succeeding without the Lord's help?

"You were right about my brother," Hope called out toward the kitchen as she stood folding towels in the laundry room. "And you didn't even say 'I told you so,'" she remarked. She had heard Eric come in the back door later that afternoon and reach into the refrigerator for something.

He stuck his head around the corner, peering into the laundry room to respond. "I thought I'd be a gentleman about it and keep my mouth shut," he acknowledged. "Nice change of pace, don't you think?"

Hope threw a washcloth at him, but smiled. "Very nice. Now, help me tell Harry to go home."

"*That* would be a pleasure." He leaned over to pick up the cloth, and tossed it on top of the dryer. "When?"

"Tonight. I'm supposed to meet him at his hotel at seven to look over his plans for the finances of the bakery, again." Rather than meet his steady gaze, Hope concentrated on the large Wedgwood-blue bath towels she was folding.

Eric was comparing the color of the towels to the

blue of his wife's eyes. He wished she'd look up again. "Tonight?"

"I tried to tell him I'm not interested in the deal, but he's not one to give up easily. At least not when there's this much of someone else's money involved," she added. Then she looked up, meeting the disturbing gaze she'd been trying to avoid.

And Eric smiled. He'd been right: the colors were not exactly the same. Hope's blue was lighter. Prettier.

"I'll go over there at seven and explain the situation to him, but he might not believe you sent me." He took a sip of the lemonade. "Do you want to come along?"

"I think I should. I'd like to get this resolved tonight. He's already mentioned it to the girls, and they were both crying about it this morning. They thought we were moving away from here—from you." Eric's eyes seemed to darken at the gentleness in her voice, and she gave him an uneasy smile. "I had a difficult time assuring them I wasn't going to do that to them."

"Or to me," he remarked. "I don't want you and the girls going too far away. Ever."

Hope lowered her eyes to look again at the stacks of laundry she'd folded. She tried to think of something to say to break the awkward silence. "I drove past the house today."

"Mmm." Eric took another drink. "And you're

sorry you did?'' he asked with an understanding smile.

''How d'you know?''

''As the saying goes, 'Been there. Done that.''' Eric shook his head as if mystified by what he was about to say. ''I hardly recognized the place, Hope. It's not even slate-blue anymore. It's this awful shade of green.''

Hope nodded in immediate agreement. ''And everything's gone. Even our lilac bushes out back. Gone. And to think of all the hours we put into the landscaping....''

''Yep.'' He gave a sad laugh of incredulity. ''They even took out the pear trees we planted beside the garage.''

''I know,'' Hope responded, her eyes wide with astonishment. ''And all the painting and remodeling...why did they bother buying the house, if they didn't like anything about it?'' Their home was gone. There'd be no going back. Had she thought they might?

Eric shook his head again and stared thoughtfully at the drink in his hand. ''We wouldn't have sold to them if we'd known what they were going to do to the place.'' He returned his dark gaze to Hope's face and her faintly pink mouth now turned down in an unhappy frown. ''It doesn't look anything like the home we loved.''

Hope swallowed and looked away. So little remained of the life they had shared. Could they find enough love to begin all over again? Her half of that question was easy. She was hopelessly, unequivocally in love with her husband. She returned her attention to him—to his eyes, his mahogany hair, his tall stature. He could be deceptively calm, as she knew too well, but in this moment she saw only honesty in him—and regret, and uncertainty. The same things she was feeling. Maybe all they needed was time…and forgiveness. But was there that much forgiveness in him? Suddenly, Hope wasn't sure she wanted to know. Struggling to think of something to say, she lowered her gaze to the glass he held in his hands. "How's the lemonade?"

"Good," he answered quietly, a little puzzled by her sudden change of mood. Then he held his glass out to her. "Want a drink?"

She put the cold glass to her lips and tasted the sweetness. She hadn't shared a drink of any kind with him since—she couldn't remember when. It was such a simple thing, and yet personal enough that she found it uncomfortable. After one sip, she handed the glass back to him. "Pretty good," she remarked.

"I'll get some for you, if you'd like."

"No, thanks. I'm going upstairs to put away this stuff." She picked up the stack of towels and turned to go, but Eric was standing in the small doorway. Walking past him would mean brushing against his left side. She raised her eyes to him in silent request, expecting him to move. But he didn't.

Instead, he reached out and touched her, brushing her cheek tenderly with fingers still cool from the glass in his hand. That wistful look in his eyes caused Hope's heart to leap into her throat. She blinked back tears and looked down at the towels in her arms. If he wanted to kiss her, he'd have to say it. She wasn't about to melt into his embrace again as she had last night.

Eric's thoughts went to the source of help he needed. *Lord, help me do something right in her eyes for a change.* Prayer. Just offering a few simple words felt so right. He wondered suddenly how he'd allowed so much time to slip by without it. "Hope, could you find someone to watch Beth tonight when we go to see your brother?"

She glanced up at him. The teenager that lived next door had watched Beth many times before. Hope could ask her to baby-sit. But... "Why?"

Eric wasn't sure where he was going with this idea, but he felt almost compelled to suggest it. Maybe it was what God wanted him to do; he couldn't be sure. Or maybe it was just his own heart longing to go home—if such a place still existed. "Would you go to dinner with me afterward?"

Uncertainty settled over Hope like a cloud. An evening alone with Eric. How could she be so afraid of something her heart wanted? Maybe because she'd lived long enough to know dreams and reality didn't always come neatly together because of wishful thinking. That she was certain of. On the other hand, occasionally they did. "Yes," she answered softly.

He nodded without smiling, and withdrew his hand, moving it away from her face and sliding it into his pocket. "We can talk."

There was a seriousness, an intensity in his expression she'd not seen lately, and she wondered about its origin. She'd prayed for him, more and more as the days went by. Prayer changes things. She believed that. Maybe it would bring her husband back to the faith he'd left. It could, if he'd let it. So many things could change.

Eric stepped to the side, allowing her passage through the doorway. He watched her walk away until she disappeared from view. Then, glancing toward a kitchen window, he saw the threatening storm clouds that darkened the sky. He was so tired, he thought, of watching her go. A homesickness beyond words swept over him. He didn't live the life he should, he knew that. He'd disappointed God. He'd alienated the only woman he'd ever loved. The Lord would forgive him, accept him as a son. Reconciliation was the resounding message of the Bible—even when we are quite sure we don't deserve it.

Eric's eyes misted with tears. Take one step toward the Lord in sincerity, and He'll run to meet you. Just as the father welcomed home his prodigal son. Eric knew that. But reconciliation required two parties to move, each toward the other. And in his marriage, Eric was only half of the picture. The rest was up to Hope. He wondered if that's how God felt sometimes when He looked down on us. He watches and waits to see us take that first step, so He can span the distance.

Placing his lemonade on the table, Eric picked up the truck keys he had tossed on the counter and headed out the back door as rain started to fall.

Chapter Seven

Eric walked into the kitchen to find Hope standing by the sink, arranging colorful tulips in a crystal vase. She looked up when he entered the room.

"Hi," she said as casually as she could manage considering her nervousness. There was a silly, schoolgirl feeling she didn't like fluttering through her stomach, almost as though this were their first date. "I didn't know if you were going to be ready in time. I heard you come back from the office a little while ago."

"I wasn't at the office," he said. He'd have to tell her—she deserved to know about decisions this big. "I went over to Adam and Angela's house again for a while."

Hope looked away hastily. She knew Eric had a way of reading emotions in her eyes, and she had no desire for him to know the vulnerability she was feeling right now. "Are things okay with them? With Nathan, I mean?" She cleared her throat awkwardly as she continuing working with the red and yellow flowers at her fingertips.

"Yes, I think so." Eric shrugged. "Nathan wants to go to a different college than the one his father attended, and that was acceptable to Angela and Adam. Understandable, too, I would say."

Hope nodded in agreement and glanced at her gold wristwatch. "It's getting close to seven o'clock. I guess we should go." She set the vase on the table. "Your mother loves tulips. Maybe she'll be home tomorrow to see these."

"Maybe, and maybe Cassie will, too," Eric added.

"I hope so," she replied. "She was certainly disappointed when Dr. Lewis decided to keep her overnight. I was with her this afternoon when he came in and told us we'd have to wait one more day, but she still wants to stay there alone again tonight, since Trudy's working."

"We can stop in to say good-night to her on our way home. Maybe that will help." He paused, glancing at the pale peach top and matching skirt Hope wore. She looked soft and lovely. "You'd better take a sweater. It's still cool sometimes late in the evenings."

Hope reached for her purse and the blue sweater she'd worn to Harry's room earlier that day. But the scent of cigarette smoke lingered on the garment, so she exchanged it for the cream-colored linen jacket she had left on the hook by the back door.

"You look very pretty tonight," Eric commented, and the satisfaction in her eyes was unmistakable. She was glad he noticed.

"Thank you. We should probably go."

Eric picked up his keys and opened the door, ushering her out ahead of him with a gentle touch to her elbow. "Beth didn't mind going next door for a couple of hours?"

"Not at all. Lora's a great baby-sitter. Beth enjoys being with her," Hope answered. "There have been times I don't know what I would have done without Lora's help."

Within moments, they were seated in Eric's truck, heading toward downtown. Eric looked amused when Hope told him their destination.

"Harry doesn't do anything cheaply, does he?" he commented at the mention of the luxury hotel. "If he has a dime, he spends it."

Hope smiled wryly. "He's always been that way, even as a child. The problem is, if he had *my* dime, he'd spend it, too. Without asking."

"You know, I really don't want to argue with him, Hope. I'd like to explain that you don't want in on his investment ideas—and leave it at that. Pure and simple." He eased the vehicle through the early evening traffic as he spoke. "Do you think that's possible?"

"I don't know," Hope answered honestly. "Harry's very determined, stubborn, self-centered, obstinate…and hardheaded."

Eric's laugh took her by surprise. "What's so funny?"

"You missed your opportunity to say he's like me," Eric replied. "Don't tell me you didn't at least think it."

"No, I really didn't," she began, then grinned. "But, come to think of it, you are determined at times. And definitely stubborn. Now and then."

"That's all?" he asked, giving her a sideways glance of skepticism.

Hope sat there, her fingers clasped together in her lap. She studied her handsome husband in that chocolate-brown shirt he wore that exactly matched the color of his eyes, and she considered the answer she'd like to give him. "No, that's not all," she responded. Dare she say what she really thought? What did she have to lose? Moving restlessly in her seat, she turned her gaze on the passing view outside her window. "You're kind and gentle. Wise, unselfish, honest. A little too proud once in a while, but always caring, giving…loving." And, unbearably attractive, at times, she thought. Like now. Hope smiled. She'd keep the last part to herself, she decided as warning bells went off in her head.

If he had no similar thoughts of her, she was in troubled waters.

Eric didn't respond immediately, which didn't surprise Hope. That was the way he dealt with uncomfortable situations sometimes: delay tactics.

They were in front of the hotel by now, and Eric pulled into the first parking space he found in the garage beneath the building. It was dark and quiet when he shut off the engine and turned to his wife. "Hope, I don't know what to say—"

"You don't need to say anything," she answered with a bittersweet smile. She met his direct gaze with some effort. "You asked what I thought, and I told you." Then she reached forward to adjust his crooked tie with a familiarity long abandoned. "There's no response needed."

Eric reached for her hand, stopping her nervous action by covering her warm fingers with his own. "You're the woman I want my daughters to be when they're grown, and I don't think there exists a higher compliment than that. But with us, Hope, you've got to let me know what you're thinking, what you're feeling. And I need to know *where* those feelings are coming from. We've lost all that—and more." He paused, then raised her hand to his mouth, brushing the back of her fingers with a kiss before releasing them. "It's been a long time since you've let me inside that pretty head of yours."

Hope smiled as Eric's gaze lowered to her

mouth, then raised again to meet her eyes. "I know," she said. "I have my reasons."

"And I want to know them," Eric replied. "I need to, Hope."

She looked away from him to stare blankly at the concrete wall of the parking garage. He needed what she'd known he'd need. What the Lord had shown her he'd need. More than she was ready to give.

"It's seven o'clock," Eric said when she did not answer. "Harry will be waiting."

She nodded and reached to open the door for herself. The silence of the walk across the parking lot was broken only by the *click* of Hope's heels on the floor. They were soon on an elevator, and then knocking on the door to Harry's suite.

"Hey, sis, come in—" Harry started as soon as the door opened. Then he saw Eric standing behind Hope. "So, you couldn't do this on your own, huh?" he asked her in a disgusted, angry voice. "Or did Eric insist on coming with you to keep tabs on what you're doing with your money?"

"I'm here because Hope wants me here. And, quite frankly, in dealing with you, I think she needs all the help she can get, Harry," came Eric's brief, but firm reply.

"Then she should probably find a better source of help than the man who abandoned her."

Eric glared at his brother-in-law. "I did *not* abandon her," he retorted as Hope stepped inside the room. "There isn't anything I wouldn't do for your sister—but the problems between Hope and me are none of your business." His sharp voice lashed at his brother-in-law, and Hope realized how bad an idea this had been—bringing these two men together. She had to do something quickly to keep things from reaching boiling point.

"Harry, please just shut up and listen to me." Her complexion paled with anger. "I don't want anything to do with the bakery. That's between you and our parents."

"And Hannah," Harry added. "At least our sister is wise enough to be investing."

"Good, fine then. You, Hannah and our parents. I'm not interested in it. The girls and I are doing well enough right here now. Just go back to Missouri, make your deals and be happy. All right? You don't need me."

"No, but he needs your money," Eric snapped, and Hope shot a disapproving look his way. If there was anything they didn't need, it was more antagonism—in either direction.

"But he's not getting any of it, so let's just go," Hope said, hoping to end this scene.

"Why don't you just let *him* go?" Harry asked her with obvious contempt, his eyes blazing with rage. "Or don't you think you could quit hanging on to him long enough to make a decision on your own?"

"Harry, that's enough!" Hope threw the words

at him. "I made my decision earlier but you wouldn't listen to me. I thought maybe you'd listen to Eric, but I guess I was wrong."

"He won't listen to anyone's ideas but his own," Eric pointed out. "You'd be better off if you stayed away from him entirely, instead of letting yourself be disappointed in his motives every time he shows up wanting something."

Harry was quick to respond. "I've listened to all I want to hear from you, that's for sure, Eric. Now, it's my turn to order you out."

"I will gladly leave the premises, as soon as you agree to leave Hope alone," Eric countered. "She has no interest in your financial dealings—"

"You left her. You're the one who made things difficult for her. All I'm offering is a chance to make things better—something you are apparently unwilling or unable to do—"

"What's that supposed to mean?" Eric's temper flared. "Financially? You think you can offer her more security than I can?"

"Well she's certainly not done so great on her own," Harry said sharply.

Hope was glad Harry didn't actually know how much money she had in C.D.s at the bank. He only assumed there'd be enough for what he wanted, but apparently hadn't found a source of information into her finances through his friend at First Choice. Where was that Ken fellow, anyway? She glanced behind her brother, but saw no one else in the room.

"I thought you said someone else would be here, too. That banker friend of yours."

"He couldn't make it tonight," Harry replied. "I was planning to ask you to reschedule."

"She's not rescheduling anything." Eric's impatient, clipped response was out before Hope could even open her mouth. "She's leaving here with me, now, and you're going to stop bothering her."

"If she came to Missouri with me, she could afford to give up teaching, be home with the children more. Can you offer her that?"

"She wouldn't be home with the girls. She'd be in your bakery at 4:00 a.m. making doughnuts or icing cakes while you'd be doing only God knows what. Hope, let's get out of here." Rage licked at the edges of Eric's control. He hadn't been in a fight for years, but suddenly he wanted to reach across the room and grab Harry Ryan by the collar—all the while knowing it wouldn't set well with Hope, or the Lord he'd recommitted his life to only hours earlier.

"Don't think that Hope will always be there for you, Eric," Harry warned with a forced smile. "When my wife left me, I thought I'd always love her. But the years have gone by, and life goes on. It will for Hope, too, someday. You'll see. And who knows? Maybe she'll marry the *right* guy next time."

Eric's blood ran cold. He didn't dare allow himself to reply. He moved methodically across the room, reached for Hope's hand, and, tugging his startled wife, stormed from the room. Harry stood staring at them, his mouth hanging open in surprise.

"Eric? Are you all right?" Hope asked as she kept pace with his long strides while they headed for the truck.

"Just fine," he growled as he opened her door and allowed her to climb into the cab. "I either had to get out of there or explode from anger. He's got more nerve than any other human being I know. I can hardly believe you're actually related to him." Eric shut her door and entered the driver's seat quickly. "How have we put up with him all these years?"

"Because he's my brother. That's how. I love him, Eric. I know he can be a real jerk sometimes, but he watched out for me when we were kids. That kind of bond runs deep."

"Apparently, deeper than I can understand," he retorted. His truck started up, and he headed through the downtown section of the city, rubbing his neck to loosen his tense muscles. He hadn't felt that kind of anger at anyone for years. Not since he'd decked some second-stringer on Hope's golf team for making a crude remark about her. That had been many years ago, he recalled as he maneuvered through a heavy flow of evening traffic.

"Well...I'm sorry I dragged you into this. Harry

is my problem. I should have handled it on my own."

"You can be a strong-minded woman at times, Hope, but—no offense intended—you're no match for Harry. Trust me on this."

Hope looked over at Eric, studying his profile as they moved along the well-lit streets of the city. She did trust Eric, with almost everything. *Almost.* A soft sigh escaped her.

"Are you tired?" he asked, noticing her solemn expression. "I thought we could get something to eat—that is, if you're interested?"

"I'm always interested in food," Hope remarked. "But maybe we should get back home to Beth."

"Beth's fine with the sitter. I think a nice dinner with you would more than make up for having to see your brother," he suggested. A hint of a smile played at the corners of Eric's mouth as he looked at her through the shadows, and Hope smiled back. Eric found himself flooded with feelings that had never been far from the surface. He loved her, now more than ever. And he wanted her back in his arms, where she belonged. Tonight and every night. Eric returned his eyes to the road that stretched before them. They were a long way from memories of yesterday.

"There's the restaurant." He motioned toward the brick building with wrought-iron fencing around the front. "Raphael's."

Hope nodded as they pulled under the awning for valet parking and left their vehicle. She slipped her arm comfortably through Eric's, and they approached the front entryway.

"I'll bet that kid hasn't parked many pickup trucks here this evening. He looked kind of disappointed."

Hope answered with a gentle laugh. "Sorry, Eric, but I think he prefers driving the convertibles and sport utility vehicles."

"C'mon," he said, placing a warm hand on her forearm. "People who drive trucks need to eat, too."

"It's okay. I'll order for myself," Hope said after reviewing the menu. She'd grown accustomed to fending for herself lately. "I'll have the fried perch, baked potato with sour cream and a tossed salad with French dressing."

"And to drink?" the waiter inquired.

"Lemonade would be good," Hope answered, and looked toward Eric as he ordered a surf-and-turf dinner with a large iced coffee.

"Still drinking too much caffeine?" Hope felt a warmth flow through her as she teased Eric the way she had in earlier days.

"I'll always drink too much caffeine, Hope," Eric assured her. "It's part of my daily routine."

She shook her head. "Some things never change."

"True enough." He sat back in his chair in a more relaxed position, his hands folded together in front of him. "Well, I think we convinced Harry that you don't want in on his deal-of-the-decade."

"I couldn't have done so without your help, you know," Hope added. She studied the attractive characteristics of her husband's face. His eyes and brows were dark even against his sun-bronzed skin, and his smile was wide when he chose to offer it. There had been a certain inherent strength in his features that had been magnetic to Hope, first as a girlfriend and then as his wife. Eric had been sure of himself, of life in many ways. And as much as she missed that in him now, she was finding herself equally attracted to the uncertainty and insecurity that had plagued him since Cassie's accident.

She realized neither of them had spoken for several moments. "So, dinner together is a nice idea," Hope said. Or, at least, it could be, she thought. It would take a little time to see how it actually turned out. "I haven't been to this restaurant before."

"Neither have I," Eric replied. "A new place seemed like something we needed."

Hope nodded and looked down at the small china bowl holding a large serving of salad greens. She was about to bow her head in silent prayer when Eric extended a hand across the table. Hope's eyes flew open with surprise. "You're going to pray?" she asked as if she'd never seen him pray before in her life.

He laughed quietly, his dark eyes flickering with humor. "I'd like to try, if you don't mind."

"Mind? No, I'm just…surprised. That's all," she said, trying not to feel incredulous. She reached out, allowing his strong hand to clasp hers firmly.

"It's been a while, but I have prayed before," Eric remarked with gentleness. "I think I can do so again."

Hope nodded before they both bowed their heads.

Eric's words were low, quiet and a bit unsteady as he made his way through the awkward moment. "Father, we thank you for this meal and for this opportunity for us to share it together this evening. Amen."

"Amen," Hope added softly. Then she raised her gentle blue eyes to meet his gaze. "Thank you."

Eric looked at her hand as he released it. "For praying?"

"For being respectful to me, for knowing I would pray so you took the initiative," Hope replied. "I appreciate your thoughtfulness."

Eric's eyes brightened with satisfaction. "I didn't do that for just you. It was for me, too."

A puzzled look came over his wife's face as she waited for his explanation. Apparently, something had changed.

"Hope, earlier today, after we talked about seeing the house, I went for a drive."

Hope waited for him to continue. "And…?"

"And I ended up at my sister's house, as I mentioned earlier," Eric said. Then he cleared his throat roughly. "I picked up Adam, and we drove around talking for a while. Until we parked in front of a church. Our church."

Hope swallowed and watched Eric's eyes spark with some indefinable emotion.

"You know, God's forgiveness is unfathomable…" he began, before his unsteady words trailed off.

Hope's eyes filled with tears, and she reached across the table to touch his hand—the one that still wore a wedding band. "He loves you, Eric. He always has. He just wants to be a part of your life again."

Eric nodded. "I know." He took both her hands in his. "I know."

She nodded, looking at him for a long moment. His ebony eyes seemed gentler than they had in ages. Kinder, warmer. And filled with possibilities. "Maybe you could come to church with us sometime. The girls miss having you there with them."

"That's one of the things I want to talk to you about." But as Eric began to explain, their waiter returned with the main courses and set heaping plates of fried perch and shrimp, clams and steak in front of them.

"Maybe we should eat first and talk later," Eric suggested. He hadn't decided exactly what he was going to say or how he was going to say it. He just knew he wanted to share all the dinners of his life with this woman he had married. It might take a while to work things out, but they could get there. He saw that truth somewhere in the depths of those crystal-blue eyes that were viewing him so cautiously at this moment.

Hope was wary, and just plain scared. Could Eric love her again the way he once had? And would he still love her, if she told him everything he had the right to know? She'd asked the Lord to help her with this more times than she could count. Maybe a messenger angel would be useful for this situation, she thought. But, not expecting to see one anytime soon, she decided to try it on her own. "Eric, there's something..." she began, and then hesitated.

He studied her face and saw a shadow of pure misery that darkened it briefly. But she didn't continue, and he let the moment pass.

"Eric? Hope?"

They both turned to look in the direction of the familiar feminine voice.

"Hello, Angela," they greeted her simultaneously. "Adam." Eric stood up and reached out to shake hands with his brother-in-law, then his nephew. "How ya doin' Nathan?"

"I'm fine, thanks," the boy replied.

"We're here to celebrate a decision we've made," Angela stated. Her dark hair framed her face nicely, and Hope noticed how much happier she looked tonight than she had earlier that day when they'd spoken.

"It must be something good," Hope guessed. "Can you share it with us?"

"Definitely. Nathan? You want to tell them?" Angela prompted.

"I'm going to college this fall in Wilmington," Nathan pushed away the lock of brown hair that had fallen across his forehead. "Instead of Trinity."

Hope and Eric smiled. "That's a good choice, Nathan. They have a great school there," Eric commented, and Hope was quick to mention a few of the positive remarks she'd heard about that college over the years. Without saying it, they both understood the motive behind their nephew's choice. His decision certainly seemed like the right one to both of them, considering the reputation his father had left behind at Trinity—footsteps in which Nathan did not want to follow.

"You look very handsome in that sports coat and tie," Hope complimented. "You're so grown-up looking all of a sudden."

"Mom wanted me to wear this," Nathan responded with a grimace. "And I try to keep her happy."

Adam joined in. "And you do a good job of it, too, son. Let's leave these two people alone and find our way to our table. Eric, Hope, it's always good to see you both."

"Especially together," Angela said with a sly smile cast in Hope's direction.

"Would you like to join us?" Eric offered, but he was relieved when they politely refused. A family dinner was not what he'd had in mind for this evening. He wanted the time with his wife. Alone.

"Angela lacks subtlety," Eric said of his sister's comment. "She always has, come to think of it."

Hope smiled and glanced down at the huge plate laden with seafood. Her stomach seemed tied in knots just now, and she wasn't sure she could eat any of it. "I like being here like this," she said softly. Her gaze shifted to Eric's gently contemplative eyes.

"So do I, Hope," he agreed tenderly. Slowly, he extended the hand that had clasped hers earlier in prayer, touching her arm with warm fingers. "I want us to do this again—soon...."

His words trailed off, but Hope understood. She gave a gentle nod of agreement. The Lord could help them find their way back to each other. But would He also give them the grace they'd need to both accept the changes they found when they got there?

Dinner might have been delicious. But Hope couldn't render an objective judgment; she was concentrating too much on the conversation. When the discussion eventually took a turn toward business, Eric's spirits lifted considerably, which pleasantly caught Hope by surprise.

"So, things have improved?" she asked.

Eric beamed, like a kid with a secret to share. "Yes, very much so. A single day can make a difference."

"What happened?" Hope asked as her eyes lingered on his almost boyish expression. He looked younger, freer than she remembered seeing him in months. And a pang of envy was Hope's first response. She wanted that, too. To feel young again, free again. With Eric. "Did you sell that apartment building?"

"We have a contract on it. A good one," he remarked. "These people actually have the money to swing the deal. And there's another sale under way that will benefit us all in the future."

Hope smiled. "I'm glad. Not just for the money to be made—but I mean, I'm glad for you. It's not like you to be so down, so unsure of things. And you've been that way lately."

"Well, Lord knows we've had plenty of things to be unsure about this past year. It's kind of hard to ignore any of them."

She nodded. "But," she said, suddenly feeling very optimistic herself, "Cassie will be home tomorrow. She's feeling great, although she was disappointed about not being released today. And your parents may be here as early as tomorrow, too, your father said when he called. Thank God your mother is doing as well as she is."

Then it dawned on her. Once her mother-in-law

came home, safe and sound, would Eric leave? The question must have registered somewhere in the depths of her eyes, because she saw Eric's steady gaze falter. She watched him avert his gaze to the coffee set before him.

"Hope—" he said, then stopped. "There's something I need to show you. Are you finished with your meal?"

She nodded and wiped her mouth with a linen napkin, wishing she had time to reapply some lipstick.

Eric stood up and pulled out his wallet to leave sufficient money for the waiter. Then he extended a hand to Hope, which she gratefully accepted, and they exited the restaurant hand in hand.

"Let's go for a drive," he suggested. "There's someplace I want to take you."

Hope shot him a curious glance. "Someplace new?"

"Not exactly," he remarked with a teasing lift of one eyebrow. "You'll see when we get there."

The valet brought the truck around, and soon Hope was seated inside. Eric glanced down at the extra keys he'd recently added to the key chain in his hand. *Lord, if I'm making a mistake, let me know. Now,* he silently prayed as he walked around the truck to the driver's side.

His decision had been sudden. He wasn't at all sure this was the best choice, but it was the only way he could think of to prompt Hope to open up to him—to tell him whatever it was he needed to know. The idea had occurred to him during dinner when he'd thought about moving out of his parents' home, and away from his wife and the girls. He didn't want to leave that house unless they went with him, but he knew he couldn't ask Hope for that until they'd dealt with whatever stood between them—once and for all. Maybe this was the way to do exactly that.

Soon his keys were in the ignition, and they were on their way, with Hope smiling happily beside him in the passenger seat—trusting him more than she'd think he deserved once they reached their destination. Of that Eric was certain.

They shared easy conversation about Cassie and Beth, talking about some of their comical antics over the years. The stories made the drive seem shorter, but they also eliminated time for Eric to reconsider this move he was about to make. It was bold. And risky. And he hoped it was prompted by the Lord. Without His help, confronting Hope's fears would be unthinkable.

"Where are we going?" she asked with a friendly smile. It felt good to feel happy again, to be with Eric this way—with a sense of adventure, a feeling of togetherness she was sure she'd never find with anyone other than this good-looking husband of hers. He guided his truck into a gravel parking lot. Then Hope looked away from Eric's suddenly serious expression to their secluded surroundings, and her smile faded. "The pool?" she breathed. She'd not been here since the day an emergency squad had transported their daughter from here to the hospital that had become her home for the weeks that followed. "Eric, why?"

Without responding, Eric got out of his pickup and walked around to open the door for Hope. "The owners are interested in selling."

That was a relief, Hope thought as she slid off the truck seat and placed her feet firmly on the ground next to Eric. This was a brief look at a piece of real estate. She'd gone with him to see properties he was selling many times before, and they never stayed long. Maybe they wouldn't even need to go inside the gate. Wrong, she realized as Eric jingled the set of keys in his hand. They'd be going in. "You're selling this for them?" she asked, motioning toward the facility.

"Yep," Eric replied. He unlocked the front gate and pushed it far enough to the right to usher Hope through the opening, his warm hand pressed momentarily against the small of her back. Then he turned to shut the gate behind them, and to flip on an overhead light to dispel the darkness that was settling in around them.

Hope's breath caught in her throat for a moment as the sights, sounds and scents of the familiar pool swept over her. Raising a hand to her throat, she touched the small gold cross, a gift from Eric sev-

eral years ago, which hung there over the peach
tank top she wore. The concession stand was
brightly painted in a rainbow of colors, just as it
had been two summers ago. There were round,
white tables surrounded by chairs, plastic and ag-
ing—probably the same ones Hope and Angela had
sat in during plenty of lazy hot summer afternoons
when their children were very young.

"How could I have been so wrong that day?"
The question haunted Hope, even now—especially
now—as she inhaled the clean scent of chlorine.
How could she have made a mistake that had
caused her daughter to suffer so much and, at the
same time, stolen a friendly summer haven they had
all enjoyed? Was swimming out of their lives forever? Or was it just swimming *here* that she
couldn't face again?

Then it occurred to her that Eric hadn't offered
any comment. She looked back at him where he
stood close to the concrete wall that encircled the
picnic tables, watching her.

"So…you're selling this?" she asked.

Eric nodded. Even through the shadows, his dark
eyes held hers easily. "Selling. And buying," he
added.

"What?" She blinked. She couldn't have heard
him correctly. "Buying? This pool?"

He nodded again, looking far too serious to
please Hope.

"Eric, you can't mean that."

"I mean it," he answered. "But I'm not making the deal on my own. Mom and Dad want in, and Rob and Micah are buying a share, as well as Adam and Angela." He paused. "Angela wants to take over the concession stand responsibilities, and Nathan is planning to be one of the lifeguards."

Hope was stunned. Speechless. How could he have arranged all of this without her knowing a thing about it? She felt so uninformed, so left out. "Eric, I—"

"This has been in the works for a couple of weeks. You've been so caught up in everything that's been happening with the girls and your brother's visit to pay much attention to what I've been doing," he explained, almost as if he could read her thoughts. "That's how I pulled this deal together without your knowledge. That and a little help from the family. I asked them not to say anything to you about it. Not yet, anyway."

"But, why?" she asked, her eyes wide and questioning.

"Because I want your immediate reaction to the idea before you have time to accumulate reasons why we shouldn't do this. It's a good financial move for us, Hope."

"Eric, you can't do this. You just can't." She had no desire to be standing anywhere near this swimming pool, let alone own and operate the thing. How dare he bring her here without warning, without a hint of what he had in mind.

"I want to do this, Hope, and we need some kind of healing from the hurt we suffered here."

"That may be true," she admitted with reluctance, "but you don't have to buy this stupid pool to find it."

"You can't go on living with this guilt...or whatever it is you've carried around with you since Cassie got hurt."

"Guilt? What do you know about guilt?" Hope asked softly.

"I know plenty about it, Hope. I've made mistakes—"

"Big mistakes? The kind that can hurt your kids?" Hope winced even now at the thought of the pain she'd inflicted. Regret and fear knotted together inside her stomach to the point that she thought she'd become ill. "Not you, Eric. You're the perfect father, the perfect husband. You weren't even guilty of unfaithfulness when you had the opportunity right under your nose." Her soft-spoken words fell harshly on Eric, she knew, as she watched him frown.

"You're disappointed that I *wasn't* unfaithful to you?" He looked stunned. "Are you listening to what you're saying, Hope?"

"No, it's just—oh, Eric, sometimes it's just easier to think that another woman took you away from me than to admit the defeat of losing you all on my own." Hope shook her head. "And maybe..." she continued, "if you needed forgiveness, *my* forgiveness, for something, anything…if you'd made a terrible mistake somewhere along the way, then it would be easier for you to understand…and to forgive me.''

Eric lowered his head and raised a hand to rub the back of his neck in complete frustration as he considered his wife's words. He'd known this wouldn't be easy, but he'd not expected it to hurt so much. ''I'm capable of forgiving, Hope, but I'd need to know *what* I was forgiving first.''

But Hope shook her head. If she told him the truth, he'd tell Cassie. And then what?

They were at a standstill. A roadblock that Eric intended to break through. ''I want you to bring Cassie here. To the pool.''

''No.'' Hope's statement was short, blunt, final. ''I won't bring her here, Eric. Why would we want to bring our child to a place where she was hurt so terribly? She was almost permanently paralyzed in that dive. It would frighten her.''

''Is it Cassie who would be frightened? Or her mother?''

Hope's eyes, as brilliant as sapphires, flashed in astonishment. ''What's that supposed to mean?''

''I don't know,'' he answered honestly. ''But, somehow, I get the feeling that you're the one who doesn't want to be here. I talked to Cassie today…about buying this pool. She didn't react negatively at all—nothing like you're doing.''

The smell of chlorine had never seemed so strong

or so offensive. It was a scent Hope had been
around nearly every summer of her life, but now
she wanted away from it. And the water. "I don't
want any part in this. It's a Granston financial deal,
and I won't be included." Hope started to walk
away from Eric and all of his questions. She didn't
need this in her life.

Eric placed his hand on the railing behind him
and leaned back. "You don't have to be a part of
it. But you are a Granston, and I'd like to keep it
that way."

Hope shot him a questioning look. "Why? Do
you need my equity money, too? Just like Harry
did?" She longed to run away from here, but the
immediate depth of hurt in Eric's eyes held her feet
to the ground.

"You've accused me of a lot of things, Hope,
but this one..." He shook his head and looked
away from her. "You know how I feel about your
brother. Don't put me in the same league with
him." Lashing out at her beyond that seemed point-
less. She had made him angry, but she had hurt him
more, and they both knew it.

"Eric," Hope began, wanting to undo the dam-
age she'd done. "I didn't mean that." How could
she have compared him to Harry? Even at Eric's
worst, he didn't deserve that. "I'm sorry. I'm just
mad...upset."

"And frightened," Eric added, looking back into
her face. Frustration was mounting and he wasn't

any closer to the truth. He kept hearing his sister's words over and over in his mind. Was there something else he needed to know about the day Cassie was injured? Angela's answer had been direct. *Yes, Eric, there is, but it will have to come from Hope.* From Hope. He blinked hard, fighting an unexpected surge of emotion. When would he ever hear the words he needed from Hope?

"Eric…" She tried to start again to explain. But she raised her hand suddenly, covering her mouth to quell her own unsettled feelings. Her heart pounded furiously against her rib cage. How had the truth become buried so deeply within her? "Oh, Eric, I used to think I'd rather lose you than admit this to you. You'll never forgive me." Her head was bowed and one slender hand moved to cover her eyes as she struggled to hold back tears that came from a depth Eric couldn't understand.

What could be so terrible? There was nothing he could imagine Hope doing that he wouldn't be capable of forgiving, as long as she loved him and wanted him back in her life—and Eric had imagined plenty. But wasn't forgiveness itself the message of Christianity? Wasn't that the very truth that had led him back to his place as a believer?

Eric was slow with his movements as he took a step toward her. And she didn't pull away the way he anticipated when he touched her shoulder with a gentle hand. She lowered her head with her back still to him—and the soft crying began. Eric winced, his eyes closing involuntarily at the sound. More tears from his wife that he couldn't stop. Then he reached forward, placing a second hand on her shoulders and easing her back enough to feel the warm pressure of her body against him. Nothing felt right without her anymore. Nothing. "Hope, hon, if you tell me what's making you so miserable, we can work through it together."

Instantly, Hope reached up with one hand, touching the fingers that rested against her shoulder. "It's not that I don't need you, Eric…it's never been that.…" In that moment, Hope felt as though her heart could almost burst with love for this man from whom she kept secrets. And she thanked God that she could still allow herself to feel that for him.

Eric squeezed her shoulders as he felt the first real sense of hopefulness he'd known in a while. At least she was admitting she still needed him in her life. He had been beginning to think he might never hear those words from Hope again. "We can make it work, Hope." He hesitated. "I won't walk away. Not ever again."

But she stubbornly shook her head. "You'll go, and this time for good. And what will I do then?" She swiveled, surprising him with a sudden turn into his arms. She'd made the first move toward the comfort of an embrace, and Eric immediately took her fully into his arms, whispering soothing words against her soft hair as she buried her face in his chest.

"It's okay, hon. Whatever it is, we'll work through it."

"No, we won't." Hope spoke the words quietly against his shirt as Eric's hands slid into silky hair. He tilted her face up toward his, only to hear her whisper, "...because you'll never forgive me. *Never.*"

"Maybe you've decided to never forgive yourself, but you can't decide for me. If I want to forgive you, then I will...and I want to do that, Hope, more than anything else I can think of at this moment." Eric's heart was racing. He thought she might pull away from him, leaving him standing there with his questions unanswered—but she didn't.

"Eric..." she began between barely controlled sobs. "The day at the pool, the day of Cassie's accident..."

He waited. He'd already imagined all types of scenarios that might explain what had gone wrong that day—including Hope being with Greg Shelton when she should have been watching their children. Now, he wanted the truth. He would forgive her; he'd already determined that. Hope had suffered enough for whatever mistake she had made, no matter how grievous. He wasn't going to heap any more pain on her by being judgmental. But he wasn't sure how tough this business of forgiveness was going to be. He knew he'd need God's help, and he knew he'd have it.

Hope raised her hands to wipe more tears from her cheeks. "Angela and Heather were with us that day, and Heather was showing Beth how to dive...showing her how easy it was to do." She paused momentarily, remembering the events of that awful afternoon. She swallowed the despair in her throat.

Eric pulled slightly away from her, enough to touch both sides of her face with gentle hands and look into her eyes. "You're not to blame for Cassie's accident. Things like that happen in life sometimes. You said so yourself."

Hope shook her head, her blond hair swaying softly, and she backed away from his touch. "No, it was my fault, Eric. She shouldn't have jumped."

He hesitated, unsure what he could say that would ease this burden. "Cassie's an excellent swimmer and diver. She had been for a long time, Hope. There was no logical reason for you to be afraid of her going off the board. You can't protect the girls from everything in life." He took a step toward her, closing the distance between them, and she leaned into him as his arms enveloped her. Then she looked up into his dark face so filled with concern, and she wondered if he really believed the words he offered or if he would have said just about anything to give her peace.

"But, Eric—" Hope stopped. She'd saved the worst for last. "Cassie didn't want to dive that day." She lowered her gaze from his. "But I told her, 'It isn't going to hurt you to do one dive for your sister.''' She paused as a look of disbelief shadowed her expression. "Can you believe that? I actually said that to her, Eric. 'It isn't going to hurt you.'''

Why? he almost asked, but had the presence of mind to remain silent. Surely, Hope must have asked herself that very question hundreds of times—each time without a satisfactory answer. He swallowed back the words.

"I don't know why I did it. I guess I thought Beth might be more likely to try it if Cassie would dive, too. It didn't occur to me—the thought never crossed my mind that anything so horrible could happen…until Cassie ran toward the board."

By now, Hope's crying had stopped. She'd told him the worst of it, and he was still standing there. She looked up at her husband hesitantly through reddened, watery eyes, uncertain what his response would be to the awful truth she'd revealed. He had every right to walk away from her. How could he forgive her? She couldn't even forgive herself.

Eric needed only a glimpse of the distress in her eyes to understand it was a pain that might never be erased, and that much of her recovery would lie in his hands. His expression was grim, he knew, as he fought back the words he wanted to say. How he wished she hadn't taken the girls swimming that summer day, and how he wished she'd not prodded Cassie to dive. But it wasn't anger that overwhelmed him now; it was regret. For the accident, for Hope's role in it—for time lost over a well- kept secret that he'd had a right to know.

"You should have told me, Hope. Right from the beginning." He raked a hand through his dark hair and paused, searching for the right combination of words to give her some relief from this sorrow.

"If only I hadn't asked her," Hope whispered into the soft fabric of Eric's shirt as she rested her head against his shoulder. "If only—"

"Don't do that to yourself. Or to us." He brushed his mouth against her temple softly. "It's just something very bad that happened to you and Cassie."

"And you and Beth," Hope added in a rare moment of tranquillity. She gave a long, miserable sigh. "And our marriage."

"But if I'd known this from the beginning, it would have changed things. If I had known what had broken your heart, I could have helped you in some way."

Eric held her close, and Hope was grateful for the feeling of being in his arms. How had she gone so many months without him?

"Don't hate me, Eric. I hate myself enough for both of us," she murmured.

Eric's hands, warm and strong, moved to touch and turn her face up to his once again so he could look into her eyes. "I could never hate you," he offered gently. "You've been part of my life for as long as I can remember, Hope. Nothing feels right without you.''

Hope breathed her first sigh of relief as she relaxed in Eric's embrace. ''I meant to tell you in the emergency room that day, at the hospital...but I was afraid to say it was my fault right there in front of the doctors and nurses. They might think I was a neglectful parent—maybe even find some reason to report me to Children's Services. Then, later, when we were finally alone together, you were too angry about the treatment in E.R. for me to tell you. Then, as the hours and days went by, it became easy *not* to talk about it. Only Angela and Cassie knew what I'd done—and Cassie didn't remember.''

''You're my wife, Hope. Anything that troubles you that much, hurts us both. I wouldn't have left you—''

''Honestly?'' she asked in disbelief. ''I thought you might have left even sooner if you'd known what I'd done.''

''Hon, you didn't do anything except spend an afternoon with your kids at the pool. Cassie loved to dive. She probably would have done so without any encouragement from you if you'd let enough time go by. Do you really think she'd watch Heather demonstrate her abilities all afternoon without wanting to show off a little, too?'' He kissed her wispy blond bangs. ''You know Cass better than that.''

"Do you really think so? Honestly?" she asked with a desperation in her voice that pierced Eric's heart.

"Yes, I do," he answered, knowing she'd have to find her way through this to some kind of peace. Somehow. Some way. Then Eric remembered a scripture his brother-in-law had read to him. He pulled away from her far enough to look deeply into her troubled eyes. "There's a verse—in I John, chapter three, I think, that says that even if our heart condemns us, or makes us feel guilty…God understands, and that God is greater than our hearts. He can set our hearts at rest." He touched her chin, tilting her face up to his. "That means your heart, Hope. Yours."

The look on her face—a mixture of surprise and possibility—reflected the emotions flooding her heart. "I'd forgotten that verse," she said more to herself than to Eric. "I recall reading it back when I had my miscarriage right before Cassie's accident. Remember how devastated we were? That's the verse your mother read to me that night. I was so afraid I'd done something to cause the loss of that baby." She blinked hard. "But the Lord gave me peace about that, Eric. It was a tangible thing. It was something I felt come over me from my head down to my toes. It was tranquil…wonderful, peaceful. And I said—"

"You said that you'd always believe in God—if for no other reason than that experience that night."

"And I would. I know He can give peace that passes all understanding."

Hope's eyes brightened, lessening the sadness that had dulled them for such a long time. The remoteness Eric had grown accustomed to seeing seemed to fade, offering a hint of warmth in its place. Relief swept over him at this first sign of a sense of freedom she'd shown.

"Hope," he said with only the slightest hesitation, "we could pray right here, together." His eyes asked more than his words. Could they open up to each other again? Completely? Enough to share something as intimate as a prayer life? That would be a greater proof to them than any words could ever be.

Uncertainty caused Hope's gaze to falter. She glanced toward the shelter house. The light was dim in that area of the grounds. But, still...pray at a swimming pool? With Eric? After all this time? "I don't know..."

Eric's smile was sweet and tender, and if he was discouraged, he didn't let it show. He reached out to clasp her hand firmly in his own. "C'mon, I'll take you home."

He switched off the light before they walked silently through the gate. He released her long enough to lock it securely before recapturing the soft hand that awaited his return. A wave of love for his wife flooded Eric's heart as they walked through the unbroken darkness to his truck, the only vehicle in the large gravel parking lot. He pulled open the door for Hope, and she slid into the passenger seat. She smiled at him as she watched him close the door and head for the driver's side.

Hope knew they'd reached a turning point. Praying together. She wanted to be able to do that again; she needed to. She swallowed hard at the growing lump in her throat. It could be the most difficult bridge to cross.

When Eric climbed in behind the steering wheel and placed the keys in the ignition, Hope extended a hand toward the dashboard, touching Eric's fingers and stopping his actions. He looked in her direction with questioning eyes.

Maybe she could do this. The Lord could help her. "It's dark here, private...maybe we could pray."

Eric nodded and took her hand in his, squeezing it tenderly. "I'll start." Then one corner of his mouth lifted a little. "At least, I'll try."

Hope smiled back at him through the darkness of the truck cab, then lowered her head and closed her eyes.

And Eric, in an unsteady voice, did start the prayer that asked for help from the Lord for his wife, for relief from the unnecessary burden of guilt, for the kind of peace in her heart and mind that the Bible promises and only God could provide. Then he thanked the Lord for His healing touch on Cassie over the past two years, and asked for the forgiveness of his own doubts and rebellion during Cassie's lengthy rehabilitation. By the time Eric finished his share of the praying, Hope was crying too much to do more than nod her head and lean into Eric's arms for a few moments of comfort.

"You okay?" he asked, his voice faltering, when she pulled away from him to reach for her purse.

"Yes," she assured him, blowing her nose rather unceremoniously into the tissue she had found. "It's just so good to hear you pray again. We used to do this every night with the girls. We used to have a God-centered home, Eric. How could we get so far from where we were?"

Eric sighed. "Not having a grateful heart, for one thing. That was my mistake." He studied Hope's profile as she sat wiping her eyes. "I don't want to end up that way again, Hope. I want us to try again—to make it work…to be a family."

She nodded and stared blankly out the window in front of her. She wanted him to love her. *Her.* Not just the children or family life or the Lord. He'd said nothing about loving Hope Ryan Granston—the woman she was now.

Just then, headlights flashed across the truck as a police cruiser pulled slowly into the lot. Eric grimaced. "They're probably wondering why we're sitting here on private property like this." He pulled his wallet from his back pocket and a couple of papers from the glove box before he opened the door. "I'll be right back."

Hope couldn't help grinning to herself as she watched Eric standing just outside the truck conversing with an officer. Her husband was tall and wide shouldered, and generally carried himself with a sense of self-confidence that consistently added to his appeal. Hope caught her lower lip tightly between her teeth. She hadn't thought recently about how very much she'd been attracted to him through all their years together. And was, even now. Married life, daily togetherness hadn't taken the edge off her feelings. Only the growing distance between them after Cassie's accident had put the reins on those emotions. She wondered briefly how she and this dark-haired, dark-eyed man had created two blond little girls with skin so fair and eyes so blue. She'd thought at least one of their children would favor their father. But then, Hope thought for a moment, maybe the baby they lost would have had his father's dark characteristics. Hope shook her head at the thought. *His.* She'd always felt that child was the boy that would have completed their family.

"Thank you, officer," Eric said with a wave to the man. Then he slid his wallet back into his pocket and opened the door to rejoin Hope in the truck cab. "They were just making their nightly rounds and wondered what we were doing here." Eric's laugh was easy, carefree as he looked across the seat toward his wife. "I couldn't exactly tell him we'd been praying. Then he'd have thought we were either liars or plain crazy."

Hope's laugh mingled with his. "True— And we're a little old for the type of behavior he suspected us to be guilty of."

"In a pickup truck in a parking lot—definitely," Eric joked.

An awkward silence they both regretted hung in the air momentarily. Hope nervously cleared her throat and fastened the snap on her leather purse.

"Hope—" Eric broke off. She looked over into his darkening eyes. "I know this is going to take time...for us to get used to being back together. That is—if you're willing to try again."

She looked away and nodded, staring down at the hand that wore her wedding ring and diamond. "I do want to try. If you do, Eric." Though she agreed with him outwardly, if she'd offered what was in her heart, it would have been a resounding "no." It would take no time at all for her to love him again as much as she ever had. Those feelings had sprung back to life—if they had ever really left at all. She didn't want to need him so much. Not now, when he still had volunteered so few clues as to his feelings for her.

"So, we'll keep things as they are for now...stay at Mom and Dad's until they're home," Eric said tentatively. "Does that sound reasonable?"

"Yes," Hope agreed. "Very."

He nodded, a little uncertain of her unspoken emotions. "Then...we'll take it from there. My apartment over the office would do for us for a

while after we leave Mom and Dad's. Until we find
something more suitable—something permanent.''

Permanent sounded almost unattainable to Hope.
She gave a fleeting look of longing that Eric wished
he could keep fixed in his mind forever. There was
something between them that had never died, and
he wanted to recapture it, hold on to it forever.

"Maybe we should go now?" she suggested
softly, unable to resist the persistent urge to check
the time. Her watch indicated the baby-sitter would
be looking for them soon. And they hadn't checked
on Cassie at the hospital yet this evening. Not that
Cassie would mind being overlooked if she knew
that her mother and father were out together—
alone—discussing the possibility of a future as a
family. Eric nodded and started the engine as Hope
thought of their family. She wanted it to be intact.
She wanted them to be good parents to their children, but she longed for them to be a couple, too.
A man and a woman who loved each other.

They headed toward the house they shared, riding in an uneasy silence. Hope had a thousand
things she wanted to say, but only one she wanted
to hear. Did Eric love her?

They were passing the Granston real estate office,
which meant they were nearing their destination
and the end of their privacy, when Eric said, "Let's
go home and check on Beth, then I'll head over to
the hospital.''

Hope agreed. "Do you think we should mention this—us, to the girls, yet?"

"Yes," Eric answered with carefully guarded optimism. "I do. I think saying it to them makes it feel more real. Don't you agree?" he added, glancing at Hope's silhouette in the glow of the streetlight.

She nodded without speaking and felt Eric's eyes remain on her briefly before he turned onto their street. Telling the children would put more pressure on them to make this relationship succeed. That part was good. But the girls would expect the warm and loving family life they'd known before—and she and Eric were far from that. At least a hallway away from it, she considered as she thought of their sleeping arrangement. This could be more awkward now than it had been since Eric moved into that house. It suddenly occurred to Hope that Grace had known it would be that way. Was that why her mother-in-law had pushed them together under one roof?

They pulled slowly into the driveway as the baby-sitter stepped out onto the porch steps.

"Hello, Lora. Everything okay?" Hope asked.

"Yes, Mrs. Granston. Everything's fine. You were running kind of late and Beth was sleepy, so I brought her over here to her own bed for the night. I didn't think you'd mind."

"No, that's fine, dear. Is she asleep?" Hope picked up her purse from the seat and pulled several bills out to pay the teenager.

"Yes, last time I checked she was." Lora accepted the money and started across the front lawn toward her own home. "See ya tomorrow!"

"Go on in, Hope." Eric motioned toward the door. "I'll watch until she gets inside her house."

The night air was cool, but Hope was reluctant to go inside just yet. There was something about the chill that made her want to stay outside, close to her husband's side.

"Aren't you cold?" he asked when he noticed she still stood there. He turned and watched Lora running up the front steps of her porch and quickly in the front door of her parents' home.

"A little," she answered, "but I love spring evenings."

Eric's gaze was dark and steady, and his mouth curved into a familiar smile. "You always did."

"But, I guess I should check on Beth."

"We'll both go. If she wakes up and finds her baby-sitter gone and no one else there, she might be frightened. C'mon," he said, motioning toward the front door. Then he took her hand in his, and they walked up on the porch and inside the house together.

Hope had started to remove her linen jacket, when Eric reached for it, guiding it off her arms. "Thank you," she murmured, watching him place the jacket on a nearby coat rack. She wished he would take her hand again. But he didn't.

He flipped on some lights and looked toward the

stairway. "I guess we should go check on our daughter."

"Yes." Hope started up the stairs ahead of him. Within moments, they were standing in Beth's room, where she was sound asleep with Brown Bear in a headlock in the crook of her left arm. "Left-handed, just like her dad," Hope remarked, looking up at Eric. "She has a lot of your qualities."

"Well, only the better ones, I hope," he responded with a smile.

Hope leaned over to switch on the teddy bear night-light, and she tucked the blanket around Beth a little more snugly. "She must be having pleasant dreams. She looks happy, don't you think?"

Eric nodded. "She'll look even happier tomorrow, when she hears our news."

"Cassie, too," Hope added. She folded her arms in front of her as she joined her husband in the doorway.

"I think one of us should go over to the hospital tonight, especially since it's Cassie's last night there," Eric said.

"I agree. I'll go—"

"No," Eric interrupted. "Stay here with Beth. I don't like to see you out alone late in the evening like this. I'll say good-night to Cass for you." Then he leaned forward, brushing her temple with a warm kiss. "And I'll see you in the morning."

Hope nodded. "Good night, Eric. Thank you... for this evening."

His look was sweet and tender as he held her eyes for a long moment before asking, "What would you think about having a second wedding ceremony?"

"That's a lovely idea," Hope responded quickly, delighted at the suggestion. "We could have one as soon as your parents and Cassie are home again."

"Dad called earlier today. He said they could be back tomorrow morning," Eric explained.

"And Cassie should be home tomorrow, too. Maybe we could get everyone together on Sunday afternoon," Hope suggested.

"This is a second chance for us, Hope. I think we should have a ceremony to make it official."

She smiled. "So do I, Eric. So do I." She watched him turn to leave, and there wasn't anything she wanted more in that moment than to be Eric's wife. Again.

Chapter Eight

"**M**om, why didn't you tell us?" Rob Granston asked his mother, almost demanding an explanation from her as he, Eric and Angela stood around her bedside.

Grace smiled at Rob and shook her head. "You're my children, not my guardians. You don't need to know everything that's going on with me. But with my health, I admit, I probably should keep you up to date on that, since you three will be left with taking care of me—when the time comes."

"Exactly," Rob remarked. "And I don't want to be thousands of miles away when that time does come. Especially if it's coming soon. If you had mentioned how badly you'd been feeling, I wouldn't have even considered—"

"—Arizona. Right? You wouldn't go, wouldn't

even think of it if I was on the verge of open-heart surgery. That's why I *didn't* tell you,'' Grace stated firmly, and extended a hand to Rob.

"Exactly what did the doctor say, Mom?" Eric asked.

"The physician I saw this morning recommended surgery. He said something about a triple bypass."

"When does he want to do the operation?" Eric asked.

"Soon. Your father and I haven't decided—"

"What's to decide?" Rob interrupted. "You're not well—you need this surgery."

"Where *is* Dad?" Angela asked, glancing toward the empty doorway. "He should have been here by now."

"He'll be here. He wanted to see Cassie," Grace explained.

"He shouldn't leave you alone this long," Angela said.

"Alone?" Grace laughed. "I'm not alone! I have all three of you mother hens hovering over me, which is exactly what I *do not* need."

"Mother, please…" Angela began.

Rob shook his head and walked away from the bickering females. "And I'm supposed to be in Arizona while all this is going on?" he asked as Eric turned to join him.

"Listen, if you want to go, don't let this stop

you. Angela and I will still be here. And Adam. And Hope.''

"Hope?" Rob repeated.

Eric nodded. "We're gonna try again."

"Well, that's the best news I've heard in a while," Rob replied, placing a hand on his brother's shoulder.

"I love her, Rob," Eric admitted quietly. "I want to marry her again—I mean, have a second ceremony. Going through that formality would give us a new starting point."

"You could use a new starting point with the Lord, you know. That would be the place Hope would want you to begin," Rob countered.

Eric smiled. "I've already found that, believe it or not. It took me a while, but I think I'm back on track with Him."

"That's great," Rob remarked as he studied his brother's eyes. "I thought something had changed. You seem different, steadier...happier. Does Hope know?"

He nodded. "I've been praying about this, Rob. I want my life back—with Hope and the girls. Do you think that's a selfish prayer?"

"It's one God would honor, Eric. What could be more in His will than for you, Hope and the girls to be a family again?"

Eric exhaled audibly and shook his head slightly. He wasn't at all certain of Hope's love for him, and he didn't want their new life together to end up an "arrangement" like the one Greg Shelton had offered her. He scuffed his foot against the tile floor and he stared down at it. He wanted her fully, totally—to be loved by her, longed for by her. He was having trouble imagining spending his life with her in any other way.

"Eric?" Hope's voice sounded distant as she peeked into Grace's room, looking past Angela and Rob to see her husband standing over by the windows.

"Hope, dear, come in," Grace called out. So she stepped just inside the door rather tentatively, holding Beth's hand as the child stood behind her in the doorway. This was a "family meeting" of sorts, to discuss Grace's health problems, and Hope felt like an intruder.

"Hello, Grace. How are you feeling?" she asked quietly when she made eye contact with her mother-in-law from across the room.

"Grandma!" Beth shrieked, and broke away from her mother to race to the bed. She immediately climbed up into Grace's arms. "You're home! And guess what? Cassie's coming home today, too!"

"Beth…" Hope moved to whisk her daughter from the room when Eric stopped her with a firm hand to her shoulder.

"It's okay. Let her go," he said as Hope looked up at him with obvious misgivings.

"I'm sorry, Eric. I know Ed didn't want the grandkids in here yet—"

"Nonsense," Grace interrupted as she hugged Beth tightly. "I'm always well enough to see my grandchildren regardless of what Grandpa thinks. So, how have you been, pumpkin?"

Eric grinned and shook his head as he watched his daughter totally captivate his mother. "You heard her," he observed. "She wants Beth here." Then he moved his hand from the gentle slope of Hope's shoulder to her soft blond hair. She turned her head to look up at him, offering a small smile—enough to let him know how right his touch still felt.

The slight curve to one corner of Eric's mouth hinted that she'd succeeded in conveying her feelings without words. Then they both returned their attention to their daughter and the three other adults in the room—all of whom were staring at them.

"What?" Eric asked suddenly, glancing from Rob's grin to his mother's sly look of satisfaction and then to Angela's expression of astonishment. An unwelcome blush crept into Hope's cheeks.

"We're gonna be a family again," Beth volunteered. "We're gonna have a new house someday, too. One that will be all ours."

"That's wonderful!" Angela all but shouted her sentiments before she rushed to hug a startled Hope. "Why didn't you *say* something? I had no idea things were going so well between the two of you. Not that I ever had any real doubts that you'd get back together eventually. I just didn't realize it was happening right here—right now! I can hardly believe it!'' she added before moving on to hug her brother fiercely. ''Oh, Eric, you're such a good man. I knew you'd work this out somehow.''

Rob walked over to Angela and took her by the arm, easing her away from their younger brother. ''Give them some space, Angela. Some time. Don't overwhelm them like this.''

''Oh, Rob, don't be so unemotional.'' She smacked him lightly on the hand before pulling free from his grip. ''This is big news! Are you planning a second honeymoon?''

''No,'' Hope and Eric answered simultaneously, and Hope's laugh that followed sounded nervous. A second honeymoon, she pondered. They hadn't yet made the long journey across the hallway that separated their rooms.

''Oh, but you really should, you know—plan a nice trip somewhere,'' Angela enthused., ''Adam and I would be glad to watch the girls.''

Hope was grateful for the arm that Eric slipped around her waist, holding her close to his side in an almost protective manner. She smiled at the thought. What did she need to be shielded from, anyway? Angela's burst of enthusiasm?

''We haven't made any definite plans yet—'' Eric explained. ''—other than that we want to try again. Right, Hope?'' He glanced at her for some sign of affirmation, which she gladly gave with a tentative smile and a nod. "We're just taking it one step at a time for now," he added.

One step at a time. Hope took a quiet breath and tried to relax, while old fears and uncertainties taunted her. Could she and Eric overcome the odds and salvage a marriage that had disintegrated? She wanted to believe they could, especially under the positive influence of all this optimism. Looking to Eric with questioning eyes, she met a gaze that was gentle and understanding, instilling an undeniable feeling of rightness. And she believed. In answered prayers and possibilities. In her love for Eric, and in taking the next step. Together.

Chapter Nine

"**W**ow! It's so good to see all my stuff!" Cassie exclaimed, entering the room Beth had been using during their stay with their grandparents. Beth had taken special care to set out many of Cassie's favorite things to welcome her home. A pink musical jewelry box, several stuffed animals and a doll with long scarlet pigtails that Cassie had named "Micah," after her redheaded aunt.

"Thanks, little sister," Cassie said with a smile, and gave Beth an enormous hug.

Hope smiled at both daughters, so relieved to be able to see them, together like this, again. "All right, you two. We're goin' downstairs for fried chicken, mashed potatoes and gravy."

"Biscuits?" Cassie asked.

"With honey?" Beth added.

"Yep," Hope confirmed, directing both children out into the hallway and down the staircase. "And coleslaw, iced tea and brownies for dessert."

"But Grandma hasn't had time to cook. She just got home today. Just like I did!" Cassie stated. "And, you've been with me all morning, Mom. Who fixed lunch?"

"Your father," Hope answered with a sly smile.

"Dad can't cook food like that!" Beth remarked. Then her nose crinkled up in a frown. "Can he?"

"No, but he can drive," Hope answered, enjoying the sound of her girls starting to giggle. "So...he picked up food at our favorite restaurant. Okay?"

"Okay!" the kids agreed, and took off toward the kitchen to enjoy their first meal together in a long time.

Later, with the table cleared and leftovers put away for dinner, the girls went outside with both parents to look over the new treehouse their father had built during Cassie's hospitalization.

It was shaped like a box. A really big one. And a rope ladder hung to the ground for climbing up.

"The green roof is neat, Dad," Beth offered the moment she noticed the addition of paint. "And the little flower box by the window is cute! We'll plant something pretty in it."

"This is so cool!" Cassie exclaimed, reaching for the ladder leading up to the enclosure. But after putting her feet on the first rung, she stopped and glanced toward her mother.

Eric dropped his gaze to the ground and waited for Hope's response.

But Hope just smiled and nodded. "Go on, honey. You'll love the view."

The child didn't waste a second in scurrying up the ladder to explore the new play place, and Beth was close behind.

Hope pushed back a strand of blond hair before Eric reached out and caught her hand in his.

"Thank you," he said, studying the satisfied look in her crystal-blue gaze. "What changed your mind?"

She tilted her head to look up into the sunny skies above them and shrugged casually. "I climbed up there the other day. It's not so high."

Eric nodded. "I told you it wasn't. I'm glad you checked it out for yourself."

"So am I," she replied, returning her attention to the girls. "I can't keep them from everything in life that might harm them, Eric. I realize that. I'll try to use good judgment about when and where to set limits." She paused. "Okay?"

He nodded again. "Fair enough." Then he looked across the yard. "Here come Mom and Dad."

"Should you be out here, walking around?" Hope asked when Grace and Ed joined them under the large oak tree.

"I have to get out and do something," Grace responded. "If I watch another talk show, I think I'll scream."

"The girls and I will check out some books for you at the library the next time we're there," Hope offered, taking great pleasure in the feel of her husband's strong, firm grasp of her hand.

"Hey, Mom? Could we have a couple of old blankets and pillows for up here? And do you think you could make us some curtains?" Cassie yelled out the side window of the treehouse. "It would look more like a home, then."

"Yes, honey. And maybe, if Grandma's feeling well enough, she could help, too," Hope replied.

"Sure, I enjoy sewing. We'll come up with something to decorate that treehouse. Now, let me get up there and see how much material we'll need—"

"You're not going anywhere," Eric said. He released Hope's hand to reach for his mother's right arm, just as Ed took hold of Grace's left.

"Eric's right. You're keeping your feet planted firmly on the ground, Gracie," Ed Granston stated.

Grace laughed. "I can see I'm not going to have any fun with you two watchdogs around."

"Get your surgery over with next week, recover well, and we'll let you do whatever the doctors say you can. Those are the rules of the house for now." Ed's voice was low but authoritative, and for a change Grace gave in.

"All right. If that's the way you want it, Edward, you can cook supper, do the laundry, mop the floors..." The older couple turned to walk toward the two-story house, their voices growing faint as they neared the back door.

"I hope your mother knows I'll help with whatever needs to be done," Hope commented. "I told her I would."

"I know you did," Eric responded. "I wish they'd keep her hospitalized until the surgery's over, but that's just not the way they do things now."

"She promised she wouldn't overdo it, Eric, but I know she wanted to be home to see us renew our wedding vows," Hope said. She turned her head to see Eric's expression when she spoke of the ceremony, wondering again if he was as committed as she was to holding their marriage together. She longed to reach up and straighten the collar on Eric's soft green shirt, but instead, folded her hands in front of her.

"That's one reason I think tomorrow is the time to have the ceremony," Eric stated. "Then she'll go ahead with the surgery early next week like the doctor wants her to do."

Hope agreed. She had the same feelings Eric did about wanting Grace to move ahead with the surgery. But did Eric have any of the same feelings she had over renewal of their marriage vows? Could those words be said by him with love, as they once were? Or only with hope that love would return?

"Eric, would you care if I called the pastor who married us? Reverend Mullens is retired now, but I know he lives over in Silver Springs Apartments."

"The thought hadn't occurred to me to do that, but that's a great idea," he responded. "Of course, if he can't come, Rob could always take care of it."

Hope nodded in unspoken agreement.

"C'mon, girls. We've got things to do," Eric called to their kids. "You can play out here later."

And down they came, climbing carefully down the ladder and running toward their parents.

"You should wear your old wedding gown tomorrow," Beth said with a grin. She grabbed her mother around the waist of her coral print skirt. "You'll be a bride all over again."

"Yes," Hope answered, leaning over to kiss her daughter's golden hair. "All over again." Then she glanced up at Eric. His expression was almost wistful, and she wished he'd say what he was thinking. Was he doing only what he *should* do in reconciling with her? Or was it what he wanted, too, somewhere deep in his heart?

The next few hours were spent making calls and completing arrangements for a brief ceremony the next day at the Granston house. Hope invited their former pastor to come, and even on such short notice, he agreed to do so.

Then Hope dug her wedding gown out from the bottom of a box in which she'd stored many keepsakes over the years. She tried it on in the privacy of her bedroom, without the children around. Her fear had been that seeing it again would reduce her to tears. And she was right. The dress was lovely, still, after all the years, and she'd kept it for the girls to wear, if they chose to, on their own wedding days. It hadn't occurred to her until recently that she might have reason to wear it again. But here she was, fourteen years later, looking at her own reflection in a full-length mirror, wearing a wedding gown…that didn't quite fit. She wiped her eyes, not sure whether they were tears of happiness for what was or sadness for what used to be. In her marriage—or in her clothing size.

Just then there was a knock on her bedroom door.

"Who is it?" Hope asked quietly while sliding out of the dress.

"It's Angela. Listen, I've already ordered the food we need for tomorrow, including the cake. Let's run over to the mall for an hour or so to pick up a few other things we need."

"Come on in," Hope called out, pulling a pair of jeans and a red top from the closet. "Let me get dressed, and then I'll be ready. Although I don't know how you can pull all this together in just one day."

"I have friends in high places," Angela said as she stuck her head in the doorway, "and, where there's a will, there's a way…or something like that.''

''Or maybe you're afraid if Eric and I don't do this right away, we won't do it at all?''

''Maybe I am,'' came the reply. Then a flash of amusement crossed Angela's face. ''Just get your clothes on and let's get out of here. Our husbands are watching the kids, so this is our chance to go shopping. You probably need some new shoes or jewelry or something for this big day, anyway.''

Hope laughed, but nodded in agreement. ''Yes, I do, Angela. I need a new dress, but…maybe we're doing this whole thing too soon. I mean, Cassie just came home from the hospital. How can I leave her with you and Adam so soon?''

''Are you kidding? First of all, you've spent so much time at the hospital that you've hardly been separated from her at all. Secondly, Cassie wants to stay with her cousins to have some fun. And thirdly, she wants her mother and father back together again—*really* together again—like you haven't been in a very long time.'' Angela reached out to squeeze Hope's arm. ''Trust me. You need time alone with your husband. There's a time for everything, the Bible says. And for you and Eric, this is it. It's just a feeling I have.''

Hope exhaled slowly. She hoped Angela's ''feeling'' was accurate, because, at the moment, Hope had little feeling of her own to go on except maybe apprehension. About the future. About lost love that might never be found. And about disappointing the children—something neither she nor Eric could bear to do a second time. They were committed to trying again, and Hope prayed they could make it work.

After Angela and the others had left for the night, Hope and Eric tucked the girls into bed with prayers and kisses, then left the room in silence. They'd only taken a step or two when Hope spoke the words that had been rushing through her mind all evening. "Do you think we're doing the right thing?" she asked, tilting her head to one side to look into his eyes. "Honestly?"

"Yes," he answered matter-of-factly. Maybe too much so to please Hope, but the warmth of his smile eased some of the tension. "It's the right thing." Then he reached out and touched her cheek gently, with a tenderness in his expression that Hope needed in that moment of doubt. "We can make this work. You'll see."

Hope watched him descend the staircase to talk with his father, who Hope knew was waiting for Eric in the living room. She turned and went into her own room for the night, and, picking up her Bible from the nightstand, she knelt by her bedside, bowing her head to pray. With her face buried in a lovely pink-and-blue heart quilt made for her by her mother-in-law, she thought mostly of her marriage:

mistakes, wrong accusations, secrets kept. She and Eric had come a long way from where they were that bitter night when he left her. But they still had a long way to go.

Chapter Ten

"Eric, you need to talk to Hope," Angela said the next day at first sight of her brother standing near the front door speaking with Adam. She stopped as she neared the bottom of the staircase. "It's time to start the ceremony, but she wouldn't come down. I left her in her room, crying."

"Crying? Is she all right?" he asked immediately even as he moved past Angela to take the stairs, two at a time.

"I think she's just—" Angela started to respond but let her sentence dwindle when Eric disappeared down the upstairs hallway "—scared." Angela turned to Adam and moved quietly into his arms, burying her face in his shoulder. "They're not going to make it, Adam. I wanted so much for them to be a happy couple."

Adam kissed the crown of her head. "We have to let Eric and Hope work this out. It's between the two of them and the Lord. There's nothing more we can do."

"Except *cry*," Angela moaned.

Adam smiled and nodded his head. "I'll leave that part to you. I think you've got it pretty well covered."

"Hope?" Eric stepped inside the open door to the guest room she'd been occupying to find her sitting at the vanity with her face buried in her hands, sobbing. "Honey, what's wrong?"

"Go away, " she said softly. "I don't want you to see me like this."

"I've seen you cry before," he said gently.

Yes, he had, and only God knew how many times, Hope thought as Eric approached her where she sat in front of a large oval mirror.

"Will you tell me what's wrong?" he asked.

"I can't go through this ceremony today. I just can't," she explained without looking at Eric as he knelt on one knee beside her and touched her soft blond hair. "I'm not sure I can *ever* do this."

"Why?" he asked in a deadly quiet voice.

"Because..." she began, then faltered. "Reverend Mullens called, and he can't come. He has to go out of state to a funeral due to a death in his family."

"All right," Eric responded, his mouth tightening as he considered her words, and his alternatives. "Rob's here—he can take care of it."

But Hope refused to be consoled. "I know Rob can do this, but I wanted Reverend Mullens because he's the minister who married us. This is all wrong, Eric. I want this day to be like our first wedding...and it's not turning out that way." Not at all, she thought miserably as she remembered the excitement, the anticipation on the day they had exchanged their vows. It seemed a million years ago.

Eric thought for a moment. He wished this could be like the first time, too. They'd been helplessly in love back then. A sad smile crossed his lips at the memory. "Hope, maybe it can't be the same in some ways, but that doesn't mean it can't be good."

But she shook her head before raising it to look up at her husband. Mascara trickled down the sides of her sad face, and Eric pulled out a handkerchief to wipe the dark streaks away. Then she caught a glimpse of herself in the glass. "Look at me," she moaned. "My makeup is a mess. My hair is awful—it's too limp, too straight."

"It's fine—"

"That's the trouble with it. It's *too* fine and thin—I can't get it to do anything I want. And this new dress I bought last night—I didn't want this

thing." She looked down at the long ivory gown
with exquisite lace designs that Angela had helped
her select. There was nothing *not* to like about it,
she knew, except the fact that it wasn't the one she
wanted for today.

"It's beautiful, Hope," Eric assured her, admiring the dress. "But I thought you were planning to
wear the one you wore at our first wedding."

"I was," she said on the verge of a sob. "But
when I put it on, I couldn't get it zipped." She
hiccuped from all her crying. "Nothing is the same
anymore, Eric! I'm older and fatter, and nothing
feels right…"

Hope could hear herself talking. Her hair, her
dress—none of it mattered as much as her heart. It
was filled with love, to the point of bursting—and
all for this man kneeling beside her whose emotions
remained a mystery to her. He would do what he
thought he *should* do. She'd known him long
enough to be sure of that. They got along well, and
could make this marriage work, with or without the
love they'd known before. But Hope wanted more.
She wanted love and life and Eric—the way they
used to be. *Why can't it be that way, Lord? Why
can't we be the way we were? Ask and it shall be
given, the Bible says. Is this too much to ask? To
want my husband back? For him to want me?* If
only Eric could read in her eyes the things she
couldn't say, she thought.

"Hope, we can't go back. Things can't be the same as they were. Not after all we've been through," Eric told her. *Lord, help me out with this. Let me get this right,* he prayed silently. He'd been so determined all along that he didn't want a marriage just for the sake of the children. He wanted Hope's love, respect, commitment. He wanted back the things they'd lost. But looking into her blue eyes, now brimming with tears and misery, he knew he wanted her on whatever grounds she would accept...because he didn't want to live another day without her. He swallowed hard. "In those months alone you learned how to live without me, but I learned something, too." In an unsteady voice, he admitted, "I can live without you, Hope. I just... don't want to. There's this place in my heart where only you fit."

Her smile was immediate, and as sweet and spontaneous as he could have dreamed it might be. "Oh, Eric." Hope barely whispered his name before she went to him, sliding off the chair and down onto her knees.

He gathered her into his arms to hold her close, speaking haltingly. "If you think that...maybe someday...you can feel at least part of the love you used to feel for me—"

"But I already love you, Eric, so much it hurts sometimes," she confessed. She stared up into dark eyes now wide with wonder—almost disbelief.

"But you didn't tell me—" he began.

She shook her head, her soft hair moving loosely about her shoulders. "I didn't think it was something *you* wanted. I thought you felt obligated to stay married to me—to try to make it work whether you loved me or not...especially now, since you've recommitted your life to the Lord. I know you, Eric, and you're the type of man who does what he thinks he should do. And staying with me is exactly what you'd think God would expect of you. I respect that in you, but I want more than that for us."

Eric watched her speak, amazed by her revelations. "But I was afraid you wanted to stay together just because of the kids. And I thought that...maybe Greg Shelton meant more to you than you've admitted." He paused. "I couldn't bear the thought of having you, but not your heart."

"Oh, Eric, no," she replied, touching his face with a soft hand. "No, I don't have feelings like this for any other man. How could I when my heart is so full of you?"

His eyes misted with tears as he hugged her and kissed the top of her head. "Thank you," he said aloud to God, the giver of all good things, and his breath stirred her hair with words. "Hope...let's start over." He spoke gently. "Marry me, all over again, and I'll try to get it right this time."

"We'll both try," she answered through tears. "And, yes, I'll marry you again, Eric."

"Here? Now?" Eric pulled away from her, just enough to look into the blue eyes shining up at him. "I love you so," he offered in a solemn, almost reverent tone. His hands moved into silky loose hair as his gaze lowered to her smiling lips. "Always. Forever."

"Eric," Hope replied, "I love you, too…so much." Then she raised up, meeting him in a gentle exchange that deepened rapidly into a lingering kiss filled with the love and longing of the past few lonely months. "I've missed you," she whispered as he raised his mouth from hers to look into her eyes.

"How did I go on without you?" he wondered aloud. "I've missed everything about you. You're so…gentle, loving, beautiful…" He spoke tender words that brought fresh tears to her that she tried to blink away. Eric smiled and reached for his handkerchief, which she gladly accepted. "You're all I've ever wanted, Hope."

"Am I?" she asked quietly. "Honestly? Still?"

Eric studied her eyes, so gloomy and wide with worry, and felt grateful to God that he'd walked away from opportunities with other women whom he'd encountered along the way. "Honestly. Still," he answered, his eyes as dark as midnight. "And always."

Hope's lips curved into the satisfied smile that Eric was watching for, and she moved with certainty back into his embrace, knowing her place was there, in the depths of his heart.

Then he was kissing her again, softly at first. Then her instinctive response led them quickly along a path they'd not traveled in a long time. Eric's hands slipped up her arms, drawing her closer, but it took more willpower that Eric realized he possessed to pull away from her slowly, leaving the lingering warmth of his mouth against her temple.

"Eric?" she whispered in disappointment. Her eyes flew open and she tilted her head back to see the passion in his gaze. A slight shiver ran through her at the sight of the smoldering depths she found there.

"There are people downstairs, hon. Waiting for us." Then he brushed his mouth gently across her forehead and gave a lengthy sigh. "We have a wedding to attend. Remember?"

Hope placed both hands on his chest, enjoying the warmth and the strength she found there. She had no desire to leave this room to join the dozen or so family members milling about the Granston house. Not now that she had her husband back again.

"But Eric, we're already married. This ceremony is a mere formality."

"Don't remind me. C'mon." He touched her forehead in another tender kiss, then stood up, pull-

ing her with him as he turned toward the door.
"We've got to get out of here before I change my
mind."

Eric paused in the doorway. Then he squeezed
her hand. "It's not easy to keep my distance from
you. It never has been." Against his better judgment, he drew her in close again and studied
Hope's suddenly solemn expression.

"And I thought you didn't love me," she said.

"You thought wrong," he replied, running an
index finger across her parted lips. Then he leaned
forward, closing the distance between them. "I
want you back in my life, Hope." Eric breathed the
words between light, teasing kisses that brushed her
mouth in deliberate torment. He saw her eyes close.
"Every day, every night...the way we used to be."
His hands moved to her waist. He could hardly believe how soft and warm she felt, how beautiful she
was. It was almost as though he was seeing her—
really seeing her—for the first time. God had given
him a new perspective, and he never again wanted
to let go of this woman he'd rediscovered.

Hope opened her eyes to meet his searching gaze.
"I want that, too," she whispered, leaning in to
him, meeting his mouth, returning his kiss...until
she wondered if a person could actually die just
from wanting someone beyond reason. Then, before
all logic eluded her, she reluctantly eased away and
stood, watching the play of emotions on his face.

"Time to go downstairs," he finally said quietly. "We'll get through this ceremony, Hope. And then I'll take you away for a second honeymoon."

Hope smiled as he held the door for her to step out into the hallway. They could use a new starting point in their marriage, and today they would have one.

"Honeymoon?" Had she misunderstood him? She'd made no arrangements for a sitter beyond tonight. "I only asked Angela to watch the kids for one night—"

Eric squeezed her hand as they started down the stairs, side by side. "Then tomorrow, Rob and Micah are taking the girls for a couple of days."

"But they're busy packing to move—"

"No, actually, they're *unpacking*. They decided against going. Micah admitted to Rob she didn't want to be so far away from family—this is the only home she's ever known. And Rob agreed with her entirely. So, the girls will be with them until Wednesday."

"Thank you for arranging that," Hope said, slipping her arm easily through Eric's and kissing him on the cheek. "A second honeymoon! Eric, I know the perfect place for us to stay," Hope added.

"I was thinking of that fancy hotel your brother stayed in during his visit."

"No, this is better," she said. "Your apartment over the office."

Eric laughed quietly as they neared the empty hallway at the bottom of the stairs. "Not exactly luxury accommodations for a second honeymoon, my dear wife."

"It has a bedroom, doesn't it?" Hope asked, glancing speculatively at her husband.

"Yes," Eric responded with an intimate smile as he placed a hand on the small of her back and guided her toward a living room full of people. "I guess we'd have everything we need then, wouldn't we?" Hope smiled up at him. Just then Angela and the girls caught a glimpse of the couple.

"Mom? Dad?" The kids came running at first sight of their parents. And Eric and Hope scooped them up for reassuring hugs.

"There they are. Hope? Eric? Is everything all right?" Angela asked, placing her cup of punch on the table and walking toward them.

"Couldn't be better," Eric assured his sister but didn't take his eyes off the lovely woman he was about to marry.

Their second marriage ceremony was soon under way, and started out smoothly. But right from the beginning Cassie's hold on her grandmother's cat, Ashley, was apparently a little too tight, which eventually caused the cat to let out a few quiet growls, and then a loud *meow*. She wiggled out of the child's arms just as Rob began reading the vows. Once free, the feline ran toward the window to climb the snow-white curtains, with Cassie and Beth both chasing noisily after her, knocking over a basket of flowers and a potted plant. Everyone looked toward the action that was taking place in the large living room.

"Just let her go," Eric said quietly, wanting to bring an end to the confusion.

But Cassie persisted. "Ashley, you get back here! You can sit through this wedding with me. It's not going to hurt you—" Then she stopped... speaking and moving. And she turned to look at her mother, who had gasped and raised a hand to her mouth.

Eric whispered a prayer under his breath and reached down to take Hope's hand in his. He'd known they'd have to deal with this, some day, some way. But he hadn't dreamed it would be now. "Cassie, hon, come here." Eric spoke gently, and Cassie, wide-eyed in sorrow, came running to her father. He released Hope's hand and knelt to catch his daughter in his arms and hold her snugly against his chest. His mind raced, searching for the right words.

"Oh, Cassie, I'm so sorry," Hope said softly in the silence of the crowded room. "I shouldn't have asked you to dive that day. It was so stupid to say it wouldn't hurt you. I had no way of knowing." Hope knelt close to Eric's side and stroked Cassie's blond curls as she spoke. "I would never do anything to hurt you. Never."

Then Cassie pulled free of her father and went straight into her mother's arms, hugging and crying. Her little head bobbed up and down against Hope's shoulder as Cassie clung to her. "I didn't want you to know," she sobbed. "That's why I've never said anything—"

"Didn't want me to know what?" Hope asked, easing away from Cassie to look into her eyes. "That you remembered what I'd said? Is that it, honey? Have you remembered all along what happened that afternoon?"

"I remembered. The things you said. The way you said them." Cassie sniffed. "You didn't mean to do it. I know you love me."

"Oh, honey, you couldn't possibly know how much I love you," Hope exclaimed, cupping her daughter's face with gentle hands. "And you don't know how sorry I am. If only I could go back and change things—"

"But we can't," Cassie said. "I thought not saying it would make it better. And for a while it kind of did."

"No, we should have talked about it. I should have admitted what a horrible mistake I'd made, and apologized to you." Hope wiped away Cassie's tears while her own continued to trickle down her face. "I'm so sorry, sweetie. Will you forgive me?"

Cassie was quick to respond. "Yes, Mom, I forgive you."

Eric stood up, blinking away tears that stung. Rob handed him his handkerchief.

"I had no idea," Rob stated quietly. "No wonder you've both been under such a strain. Why didn't you say something?"

Eric shook his head. "It's a long story."

Beth was hanging back, just close enough to see what was going on without being a part of it. Eric motioned her closer. "It will be okay, hon." He picked her up and studied her look of uncertainty. "Mom and Cassie have had a misunderstanding, but things are going to be okay now."

"You sure?" she whispered, her face scrunched up into a doubting frown.

Eric glanced over at Hope where she knelt hugging Cassie tightly. "Yes, I'm very sure," he replied, and thanked the Lord silently for this unplanned resolution.

It took several moments for everything to calm down enough for Rob to start the ceremony again. When he did, Eric and Hope repeated their vows with love and commitment evident in every solemn word they spoke. Then they returned their original wedding bands to the rightful places—bands that had been missing for less than an hour. That simple act brought immediate shrieks of delight from the two little girls who benefited most from this reunion, and tears to the eyes of every female present in the Granston household that day, including Rob and Micah's little five-year-old Liz, who cried just because everyone else around her seemed to be doing so.

Then, with their hearts filled to overflowing with blessings, Eric and Hope bowed their heads along with the rest of the family in a prayer that was offered over trays of sandwiches, cheeses, an assortment of fresh fruit and other items to be enjoyed. And, of course, there was the wedding cake, which Eric and Hope were not around to sample when the time for dessert finally arrived. They had said their goodbyes to their girls, then quietly slipped out of the crowd and to Eric's truck, starting toward the new beginning God had given.

* * * * *

Dear Reader,

Thank you for choosing my book, *The Forever Husband*. I trust that Eric and Hope's story will touch your heart the way it did mine as I was writing it. Their marriage began in the best possible way— warm, loving and centered in the Lord—but became lost somewhere in the struggles of life. It takes a lot of trust in the Lord, and in each other, before they can open their hearts again.

On their journey back, Hope must forgive herself for a mistake she made. Sometimes forgiving ourselves is one of the most difficult issues we face. But the Lord is there, wanting to show us the way, if we will let Him.

I enjoy hearing from readers! Feel free to write me in care of Steeple Hill/Love Inspired, 300 East 42nd Street, 6th Floor, New York, NY 10017.

Best wishes,

Kathryn Alexander